Fluid

A Mindspace Investigations
Novella

Alex Hughes

Fluid: A Mindspace Investigations Novella
Alex Hughes

Hughes, Alex C.
Fluid: a Mindspace Investigations Novella / Alex Hughes
ISBN: (ebook edition) 978-0-9916429-3-9
ISBN: (print edition) 978-0-9916429-4-6

The author wishes to acknowledge the following professionals for their services during the production of this book, with great gratitude:

Developmental Editor: Jesse Feldman
Cover Designer: Scarlett Rugers, www.scarlettrugers.com
Formatter: Polgarus Studio, www.polgarusstudio.com

It was eight a.m. on a normal Monday at the Mindspace Investigations P.I. office, which meant neither my partner, Isabella Cherabino, nor I had a case. In fact, cases had been all too rare, and we were running disastrously short on money. I supposed it wasn't surprising the phones weren't ringing off the hook, what with a distrusted telepath and a publically disgraced detective running the business. But we needed this to turn around quickly. The bills had to be paid.

Lately, the normally-volatile Cherabino had gone cold and quiet, nothing at all like her usual anger. That worried me.

The phone rang—or more accurately, all three phones rang, the one in the front and the other two at our individual desks.

"I'll get it," I said, and dashed to the closest one on my desk. "Hello?" I said after I'd picked up the receiver. "Oh. Mindspace Investigations, Adam Ward speaking."

"That's a terrible name, you know." A man's voice sounded on the other end of the line. His tone was calm and detached.

I was stung. I'd picked out the name myself. "Hello, Sergeant." Branen was Cherabino's boss, or since she'd been fired from the department on that brutality charge, her former boss, back when she'd been a homicide detective. I still worked part-time for him. If he'd gotten more hours approved for me, that was a very good thing. Even if he did criticize the name of my new firm.

"It's Lieutenant now, actually," he said. "You're going to scare off normals with that kind of reference to Guild telepaths."

"I'm not affiliated with the Telepath's Guild at all," I said. They'd kicked me out for a drug habit that wasn't strictly my fault over ten years ago. "You know that."

"Yes, but, the public doesn't. Anyway, I have another set of consulting hours approved for you, and a case. I'd like you to come in and work with Detective Freeman."

"Who is it?" Cherabino whispered very quietly, almost too quietly for me to have heard with my ears. The telepathy helped with that. I was a Level Eight telepath, or thereabouts, and Cherabino and I had a weak telepathic bond.

"Branen," I mouthed at her. I could have spoken to her mind-to-mind, but she didn't like that. To the phone, I said, "Happy to help, Lieutenant. And congratulations on the recent promotion."

"He's a lieutenant now?" Cherabino asked under her breath. She was feeling. . . left out, then cold, again, in Mindspace.

"Thanks for the congratulations," Branen said, after a second. Apparently I'd actually surprised him with the courtesy. Why did everyone assume I didn't know courtesy? "Can you be here in ten minutes?"

2

"I need twenty, but I can meet Freeman at the scene."

"I'll transfer you to Kalb, my assistant, for the address," he said, and I heard the sound of elevator music.

"Today's a bad day for you to go in. We have work," Cherabino said again, almost too quietly.

I put my hand over the receiver, just in case. "What work? We don't have any work, that's the problem. We need the money."

She shook her head, and I felt that coldness, that sadness from her again.

I paused. "Why are you so against this?"

She didn't say anything.

The music ended abruptly, and a younger man's voice came over the line. "Ward?"

"That's me."

He read an address out to me.

I repeated it back to him and then said, "Do you have any details about the scene or what I'm expected to do?"

"None whatsoever, I'm afraid."

"Peachy." I sighed. "Well, get the dispatcher to radio out and tell Freeman I'll meet him in front of the building in maybe fifteen minutes."

"Will do," the assistant said, and hung up.

I turned around slowly.

Cherabino's face was set in that careful blankness I called her cop face.

"Are you—" I started.

She cut me off. "Just go."

I shook my head, grabbed my coat from the back of my

chair, and started walking towards the door. "We need the money, and Freeman's going to be pissed if I'm late," I said, walking faster.

"*Adam*," she whispered.

I turned around. I could *see* the emotions rolling over her in Mindspace for one long second, frustration and hurt and deep, deep anger all at once. Then they were all gone, and that cold was back, that too-cold, too-sharp control. That hurt.

"I can't give you back your job," I said. "I wish I could. I do. But I can't. And we really need the money right now." She'd been set up by a criminal with a grudge against her; but she didn't know she was set up, and I hadn't figured out how to tell her. To her, it felt like her whole world had been taken away unjustly.

I expected anger, anger like a tsunami, when I mentioned her lost job; but instead she sat down, pulling into herself with apparent defeat. Her hurt also hurt me, but there was nothing I could do about it. Nothing.

"Just go," she said.

I took a breath, turned back, opened the door, and walked out. I couldn't do this right now, and anyway there was a crime scene to get to.

She'd go back to being her usual fiery self. Wouldn't she?

The apartment building was a tall brick-and-concrete monstrosity, like a squat troll sitting over its fellows in judgment. Not quite post-Tech-War architecture, with the reinforcements and easily defended entryways in vogue fifty years ago, but neither did the buildings have the lightness of recent architecture. In other words, there wasn't much to recommend the place except its location: three blocks from the Square, the heart of Decatur, and the MARTA station with its access to public transportation around Atlanta. It was a fine day; a recent rain meant the usually-thick pollution was lighter than usual, hardly enough to make you cough. Traffic was a steady flow here, both on street level and in the skylanes, as the tail end of rush hour moved through the city.

I met Freeman in front of the building. He was a tall guy in his late forties with a dark complexion and a scar on the right side of his face, and he always seemed tired no matter what else was going on. His boxy coat nearly swallowed him, the fisherman's hat putting shadows under his eyes.

I used to think Freeman didn't like me, and that was true so far as it went. But I'd since figured out that he didn't like many people, and that a lot of the hostility I'd been attributing to him was simply his scar pulling his face out of shape. He was a good cop, a good cop to his core, and he was happy to work with whomever and do whatever it took to keep the public safe.

I missed working police cases with Cherabino, who'd been a detective until she'd gotten fired a month ago. But I'd been called in to consult with Freeman a few times since then and it worked, even if he didn't like me enough even to give me a card for my birthday.

Freeman finished signing something with the uniformed officer in front of the building and then turned to me. "Floater in the apartment swimming area," he said, and that was it.

I read the rest off his mind, since he'd prefer not to talk given the choice. One of these days he was going to think about what it meant to have a telepath reading you. One of these days he was going to mind, I thought. But today wasn't that day.

A body had been found in the apartment complex's swimming pool area about ninety minutes ago by another resident. It was a journalist named Isaiah Jeffries. The uniforms had knocked on doors and confirmed that no one else had been at the pool that evening, so no witnesses they could find.

"Wait," I said. "Isn't Jeffries the guy who shut down the child sweatshop rings near Stone Mountain?"

Freeman frowned. "He wrote the articles. Cops did the real work."

"Even so," I said. Come to think of it, though, that was before I'd gotten kicked out of the Guild. A long time ago. "What has he been up to lately?"

"Going after the department, mostly," Freeman said. "Or trying to. He's caught a few bad apples and assumes there's more."

I blinked, not knowing quite how to take his tone of mind on that one.

"We'll investigate it by the book either way. How long do I have you for today?" he asked me, a valid question since I was part-time, dependent on department funding and Lieutenant Branen's goodwill.

"Just a couple of hours," I told him.

He thought about that for a second, apportioning his time

accordingly. We both knew I would stay longer if I needed to, but too much untracked time made the department's accountants angry.

"I'll have you talk to the woman who found him, and then you'll meet me at the scene," Freeman said. His face twisted in disgust, but his mind was thinking about the effects of waterlogging on a human body in a public swimming pool, not anything to do with me. He had some very vivid images of other waterlogged corpses in his brain, vivid enough—and loaded with smells—that I pulled back, my stomach roiling. There were some things I hated about this job, and the bodies were one of them. I fought down nausea and told myself I'd get through this. I was going to interview the woman first anyway.

Freeman opened the heavy front door for me, and I walked in, the portcullis overhead making me feel slightly claustrophobic. The lobby inside was surprisingly light and luxurious—marble floors mixed with intricate faded wallpaper, delicate ceiling tiles, and a large wooden front desk—like an updated hotel in the style of the 1940s. It was still cramped, but I could see why the residents paid extra if the apartments had this kind of luxury feeling. It didn't match the outside, that's for sure. A leasing agent with a name tag sat behind the desk, nearly doubled up on herself as she shook her head over and over. A uniformed cop stood next to her, probably a rookie by the body language, not sure what to do. I saw Freeman note the two and move on.

At the end of the lobby was a blonde woman in runner's clothes, a gym bag floating next to her on pricey anti-gravs just above the marble floor. She tapped her foot, literally tapped her foot, seemingly full of energy but unable to use it to leave. She was maybe 5'3", on the short end, stocky but strong, with a cherubic face and blunt bangs that framed blue eyes. The feeling I got from her in Mindspace was concern—and kindness. She had more than a trace Ability, I thought, but we'd get along just fine.

She "heard" my attention and looked up, moving forward to meet us. "Are you the detectives in charge?" she asked. "I'm Molly. Molly Lenore McAlexander Smith, but everybody calls me Molly. I'm an architect. I've got to be at work this morning. My boss said I can be late for this, but I can't be too late, if you know what I mean. We've got a project, and the deadline's coming up."

Freeman asked her, "You were the first to find the man?"

She looked at me again, frowning a bit, probably reading my Ability without realizing it. She wasn't strong enough to be forced to be Guild, but other telepaths were much easier to read than normals, so she'd notice me.

Hello, I said to her mind-to-mind, and, *I'm Adam Ward. Freeman here is the detective in charge.*

"Okay," she said, and moved on, probably not even realizing that I hadn't said it out loud. "I can go through this again, I mean I know you've got paperwork and a job to do, but I really need to check in with my hubby and make sure he got the munchkin to school okay and then get into work." She sighed. "I guess there's no way a run is happening today, is there?"

Freeman looked at me. "Well?" he asked me. Subtext was

that his instincts were reading her as honest and overly helpful, definitely not the killer. If I'd confirm that for him, he had other tasks to take care of through the double doors to the right, where the pool was.

"I've got it from here," I told him, in answer to the unspoken question.

Freeman moved forward through the double doors, went ahead, mentally preparing himself for what he was about to see. Ms. Smith's head swiveled as she followed him with her gaze.

"Thanks for staying and going through all the procedure," I said, largely to draw her attention back to me. "I know it can be frustrating."

She shrugged, her mind open to me but still guarded enough for public space with a new acquaintance. She had good instincts, this one. "Don't the TV shows say you have to eliminate the finder person first? I don't mind helping you check a box, but like I said, I can't stick around forever."

"Because of your project at work," I said, and smiled, to make her like me. "Yes, I heard. I'll go ahead and ask you my questions and then you can head out."

She frowned at me, probably picking up on the slight lie of the smile. Sharp one, for certain. "Sure. Go ahead and ask."

I took a breath and relaxed the smile into something more reasonable, deciding not to lie if I could help it. "You live in the building?" I asked.

"Yep." She gestured loosely in the upwards direction. "Fourth floor, 412, all the way at the end, right by the garbage chute. It gets noisy on that end. I'm four doors down from Jeffries and his wife. I think. It might be five. We're not close, but I get their mail sometimes. They used to live in my apartment, I think. Not sure why they moved. Managers have been raising the rents on newbies for years, you'd have to be an idiot or spendthrift to move."

"Jeffries?" I asked.

She frowned at me. "The guy in the hot tub I found this morning. Isaiah Jeffries. He's dead," she said. A clear subtext from her mind: *Please try to keep up, I have to leave soon. Really soon. Like, get there way before the noon meeting.* "I forgot to get my mail last night, and John didn't get it. He never gets it. He's a great guy, he just doesn't get the mail." She took a breath, and for the first time I understood that all the talking and helpfulness was her way of dealing with the body she'd found. It was upsetting to her. She hadn't seen bodies outside of funeral homes, ever, but if she talked, if she helped, maybe it would all go away and settle into normal again. "So I went downstairs to get it a little earlier than usual, and I cut through the pool on the way to the gym for my morning run. And I saw him."

"Saw Jeffries?" I prompted, when she didn't continue talking on her own.

Her eyes focused on me again, and she gave a small shake, like pushing the memory away. "Yes." She took a breath. "Yes, he was in the hot tub like I said, with a half-full bottle of whiskey next to him with three beer bottles. Real glass, you understand. At the pool. It's against the rules and stupid as all get-out to get drunk while you're in the water, but he has a bit of a reputation around here, and—"

That I cut her off for. "Reputation?"

"He likes to drink, if you understand what I mean. I don't think I've ever seen him completely sober. I guess that's what happened to him, right? He fell asleep in the tub and knocked something over or something." She pictured the scene again in her head, and I got the edge of it. She was disturbed, as she probably should be, but also had just a tinge of contempt that he'd done something so stupid in a public space. Alcoholic, she thought, in a tone of mind that stung me a little.

Just because you were an addict didn't make you stupid, I wanted to say. But instead I pushed it to the side and moved on.

"How did you know it was him so quickly?" I asked.

"Well, his head was sitting back against the back of the tub, funny angle but okay. I could see his face right away, but his eyes were open and . . ." she shuddered and looked away. "Well, it was obvious he wasn't breathing anymore. The hot tub was off and cold, but it smelled funny, like something burned. Something electrical maybe. I was pretty sure I shouldn't touch it even before I saw the sparks."

She'd felt the edge of an electrical field, perhaps. Mindspace and strong electromagnetic fields interacted in interesting ways, and some people were more sensitive than others.

"Sparks?" I prompted.

"He had some kind of thing—an electrical device next to him. I didn't see clearly what it was, all I saw was the cord as it went in the hot tub and the sparks from there to the puddle on the floor. That kind of thing could—well, it did kill somebody, I guess. I called the super and I called the police, in that order, from the phone next to the pool bathroom, and then I stuck around so nobody's child got close. I was glad I had rubber-soled shoes on, you know? I did have to call my own apartment to make sure John knew he needed to drive the munchkin to school this morning. The police took forever to arrive. Monday, I guess. The rest you know."

I chewed that over for a minute, reminding myself that her first impressions weren't necessarily indicative of what had happened, but her read seemed good. "You didn't touch anything?" I confirmed.

She shook her head, then added verbally, "No. It didn't seem like a good idea, and with the tub cold and him not breathing there didn't seem like there was a reason to do it." She considered absently whether she would have risked it if he'd been alive, and wondered. She didn't know him well, and he'd been an alcoholic, and he had brought the alcohol to the pool . . .

That last bit was all I needed to know. Only honest, innocent people asked themselves the kind of hard moral questions she was asking herself now. The guilty folks tended to shy away, and certainly not to question such things in front of cops (or consultants to the cops, in my case). I was nearly certain then that she hadn't had anything to do with the death, even by omission or influence.

"You did the right thing," I told her, and added, "Especially with an electrical hazard. You called the experts, and you kept anybody else from getting hurt. Then you stuck around to answer questions."

She met my eyes and nodded, accepting the words. "Thanks."

"I have just another couple of questions, and then you can go," I said, in a more businesslike tone.

"Shoot."

"You said you didn't know Jeffries well."

"Or his wife. Second wife, I think. There was something about a divorce attorney in one of the letters that I got a year ago, and then the new woman arrived." She frowned, looking up, thinking through what she knew. "That's about all I know. They don't come to the block parties, I just know him because of the reputation and the mail. And the occasional rumor, but it was all stupid vague stuff about the divorce."

"Did you know anything about what Jeffries did for a living?"

She thought about it, frowning. Finally she offered, "His wife now is a nurse, or something like that. I've seen her in scrubs a few times. Probably not a doctor because she always wears the ring on her hand, at least as many times as I've seen her."

"Doctors don't wear rings?" I asked.

"Haven't you noticed? The ones who work in hospitals don't wear jewelry because it harbors germs, and the ones who don't always seem to be having affairs."

That was an interesting theory. "You notice a lot of details, don't you?" I asked.

She shrugged. "People are interesting."

I tried to think of another question and came up blank. I thought she had told me everything she knew. "Well, call the station if you think of anything else," I said, the standard closing. I gave her Freeman's number and explained that I would come out to see her if she left a message.

She paused, like she was listening to a faraway sound. Then her eyes focused on me again. "I need to call my hubby just to make sure he's got things under control," she said, and picked up her gym bag, toggling off the anti-grav switch before setting it on her shoulder.

"You're free to go," I replied, and forced another smile.

As I watched her go, though, the smile fell. From what I'd seen even second-hand, this was going to be an unpleasant crime scene.

The smooth marble floor of the lobby turned to large square tiles and then to smaller rectangular tiles in front of a large double door of beveled glass, currently open. On the other side was a floor of poured patterned concrete transitioning into the formed side of an Olympic-sized pool, filled with the teal colored water of the truly high-end non-chlorine pools. A huge, domed skylight shone sunlight onto the water. It was a gorgeous pool area, indicative of real money in this building, I thought.

Halfway down the brick side wall was a large, raised hot tub, its sides tiled. At least half a dozen police personnel grouped around that hot tub, talking in low tones that echoed strangely in the space. Mindspace seemed to follow the trend, low-level thoughts like waves dashing over one another, strange echoes like the waves in the pool in front of me.

I walked down to the group, their thoughts getting louder as I went. I realized that I had dropped my guard while talking with Molly, and cautiously rebuilt my separations with the outside world, like the screen door I had taught my students to create—a transparent separation you could open or close at will.

Freeman was with the group, in charge by the body language and the deferral of the others. He saw me and nodded. "We'll need to clear the area now," he said, in a loud voice that echoed.

The others turned and saw me. Jamal, one of the techs I kept running into at scenes, made a face, but he, like the others, stepped back to give me room.

I immediately wished they hadn't, as I saw the body for the first time.

There was something viscerally wrong about seeing a person underneath the waterline, unmoving, something that bothered me far more than the circumstances probably should have. The face was puffy, waterlogged, out of shape. No bubbles came out of that open mouth, and the eyes were red and open. His long arms floated, his upper body half in, half out of the water, his head lolled to the side and underneath it. The skin was heavily wrinkled, almost pulling away from the body, and there was a visible difference in color between the darker, normal warm brown skin of his ear and side-head above the waterline and the wrinkled, lighter stuff of the face below, almost gray, like the color of a long-hidden mushroom.

The waterline of the hot tub was still, completely still, the jets long since turned off or burned out. As Ms. Smith had said, there was a smell of burning around the area, a smell that felt wrong too. Everything about this one felt wrong, gave me the heebie-jeebies in a way I couldn't explain.

My eyes fell away from the body, unable to keep up the focus on it—on him, I told myself. On Jeffries. He was a person, he'd been a person, and he deserved that respect even if the face under the water made my stomach churn and my body feel light-headed. He'd been a journalist, somebody who brought things to light. He deserved respect.

A glass bottle of Jack Daniel's, half empty, sat on the ledge behind the victim's head, along with two glass beer bottles. A dark line, like a scar, was burnt into the plastic lip of the hot tub, maybe a foot away, near his shoulder. Where it met the water line was a wavy oval, even darker black on the side of the tub, and reaching out for maybe two inches in every direction, a starburst burn. On the victim, no burn that I could see.

I asked the closest uniform, "Has someone moved him?"

"Not since I've been here," the guy said uncertainly, a rookie by the feel of him in Mindspace. "But I've only been here a little while."

"Why do you ask?" Freeman asked, looking at me and the rookie from ten feet away.

"The witness said she found him with his head out of the water." She'd also said she'd found him with three beer bottles and there were two here, but that kind of mistake was pretty common for eyewitness accounts. I took a breath, ignored the burned smell in the back of my throat, and tried to think more critically about the scene, past just the obvious.

After a second, I asked, "Where's the electrical cord?" After some thought I vaguely remembered Ms. Smith mentioning some kind of device in the water, but I didn't see anything.

"On the other side of the tub," he said.

"I took the box out after I disconnected the cord from the wall," Jamal said. Another new tech I didn't know opened his mouth to talk, but Jamal cut him off. "That's what I did. It was better to take care of the electrical hazard. It was caught up in the guy's legs and made him move. That's all that happened."

Ah, that would explain it. Moving the body was a no-no, and he was understandably defensive about it.

I took a step around the tub, so I could see what they were talking about. There it was, in a puddle of water, a plain foam-sided box with the metal shape of a compressor sticking out of one end. A broken beer bottle was next to it, having fallen out. Its cord was blackened starting a foot away from the box itself. An extension cord, also blackened, was disconnected from it, in a pile about three feet away. I was glad to see that its end, too, was disconnected from the wall near the door ahead.

"It's a cooler," Jamal said.

Something nagged at me, information I'd learned in a former case. "Don't modern electronics have a kill switch so they don't do this kind of thing when they hit the water?"

The tech closest to me, a woman in baggy scene overalls, frowned thoughtfully. "They usually do," she said. "I'll take a look at this one and see how it failed."

The rookie cop shifted, not sure what to do.

Freeman made an impatient sound. "Leave the processing to the rest of the crew. That's their job. You take a look at the evidence in Mindspace, please, and don't make the rest of them wait any longer than necessary."

At his words, the six folks, including the uniformed officer, took another few steps away from the tub. Freeman ran a tight ship, much tighter than Cherabino, something that was becoming more obvious with every case I worked with him.

I took a breath and forced down my irritation. He was right; I was the one slowing things down at this stage, even if it was pretty rude to push the point.

Freeman took a step forward, and said very, very quietly, "You look twitchy. Something I should know about?"

I'd been clean for four years now, but my last dive off the wagon was pretty public and right in front of the cops, and since then there hadn't been any secrets allowed. "No," I forced myself to say evenly. "No, it's just the scene."

He looked at me for a long moment, with that tone of mind you get in old cops, the pause where they waited for you to hang yourself or prove yourself.

"It's the scene," I said, almost an echo, just to fill the silence.

He frowned. "Seems a normal enough scene. Accidental electrocution. With the alcohol. If this wasn't a high-profile journalist, we'd be done processing already. We've got a backlog today."

"High-profile?" I asked.

He shrugged. "He hasn't done much in the last few years, but the articles he published last month against the so-called 'dirty cops' got a lot of attention. Plus he called out some city officials. Branen says it's wise to treat it like a high-profile murder until we prove accidental, and I agree. It's why you're here. We've done other cases. You're not like this. What's going on?"

"It's not . . ." I trailed off, trying to put my finger on what was so wrong. Now that my eyes were on the body, it wasn't bad enough, shocking enough, to have this kind of instinctual response. What was wrong?

A good question. The right question, I thought. I opened myself up to Mindspace, lowering my defenses just enough . . . and was hit in the face with strong emotion. "Fear," I told Freeman. "Whatever happened here, he was afraid. Fear all over, seeping into the very walls."

"So it's not an accident," the detective said, in the tone of voice that said he neither believed nor disbelieved.

"No," I said.

Freeman shook his head. "Well. You're here, I'm here. Take a look at the mind scene—without making us all wait any longer—and we'll go from there. I want you to talk to the victim's wife if we can find her."

"Did the wife see him like this? Does he get drunk in hot tubs a lot?"

Freeman made an impatient sound. He had a mental "hand" already held out, waiting.

I sighed, and complied. It was dangerous for me to do a deep-dive into Mindspace alone, into the space where thoughts echoed, emotions lingered, and people's minds propagated. All the more dangerous when a death was involved; here, I needed an anchor for a crime scene. That anchor used to be Cherabino, for a long time, Cherabino, and I missed her.

Freeman's mind was so . . . flat in comparison. Perfectly serviceable, like an old wallet, deep creases in spots, wear in spots, it did the job it needed to do promptly and without complaint, without bells and whistles.

I reached out to "take" his mental hand, a strong thought only. He'd rush me, I knew this already. I'd learned this already on the times we'd worked together before.

Right before I sank into Mindspace, I read something off the top of his mind and said it without thinking. "You're the only one Branen trusts to find the truth no matter the politics," I said, surprised, as I finally understood why Freeman had been tapped for the politically-charged journalist.

Freeman smiled, a small smile that pulled at his scar. It wasn't a pleasant expression. "Everybody here, from the top to the bottom of this crime scene, is handpicked." Most of them by him, some by Branen. Freeman had gone to the academy with Branen and been through a lot of crap with the man. Freeman didn't want to be the captain, didn't want the responsibility of moving up the ladder, but he did want respect, and the responsibility of the hard cases, the special cases, and he got that. Freeman's informal trust team had been quietly solving the touchy and the difficult cases for twenty years, without any fanfare. He expected me to do the same.

"Cherabino never knew about this team," I said, all of it hitting me.

Freeman shook his head, impatient to get me to do the read and move on with the day. Cherabino didn't move quickly; she worked too much, he was thinking. She also was a bit too unstable since her husband had died, and had never really settled. Proof of that was her conviction for police brutality weeks ago. Whether it was true or not, Freeman would never have gotten caught in a similar situation. I, in contrast, was only here because I'd finally proven that I was stable enough—for now—to add something. "I'll say it again," he remembered telling me. "You're honest, you're straightforward with me, we can deal with whatever you've got going on." He meant another fall off the wagon, if that happened. I'd bounced back twice and seemed motivated. It happened, he'd deal with it and help me bounce back again. "But you lie, you cover it up, you're going to be out."

I nodded.

"I don't have all day. Read the damn scene," he said, now.

I laughed, a hollow sound, settled back into my mental grounding. Maybe I was avoiding this. As fast as I dared, I sunk into Mindspace.

The world opened up around me, thick and dark, a place utterly and completely without light, experienced through feel only, completely without the eyes, like the echoing of a bat through the night. I settled deeper, past the shallows where Freeman's thoughts and the thoughts of the other techs sat, into the emotions left by the man in the hot tub at the time he died.

Mindspace had settled towards the body, like water draining out of the space, some lost into . . . wherever minds went when they died. What was left was pulled like taffy, flavored with fear, with a feeling of suffocation, of breathing heavy water, of inevitability. Of seeing death coming and being unable to do anything against it. That feeling, that fear, was so strong in the air, in the space, that I was nearly overcome, literally choking on the emotion.

I forced my mind to calm, forced my lungs, my throat to

relax. I took a breath, then two, then three, pulling air through my body to help ground me back in the real world. I was not choking. I was not breathing water. See, I was free. I was breathing. I was fine.

I eased into the space, looking for details. Looking for whatever he'd been afraid of. There, a frantic motion. There, a crack—the glass had fallen, the water splashed all over. Frantic, frantic, hold him under. He wasn't dying. He was struggling. He needed to die already, quick, quicker, now.

I pulled myself back from the killer's thoughts. Who was he? If it was a he at all. Sometimes I didn't get a strong gender, and this was one of those times. He for the sake of talking about it. Not very confident. A person very concerned about this, his first kill, his first murder. I felt the decision, like through a kaleidoscope, the decision to speed things up by pushing the cooler into the water. The rush of the electrical field through everything, a field in Mindspace that raised the hairs on my arm, the decision, the field, the decision, the field.

"There was someone else here," I told Freeman, up the faint line that connected me to him in the real world, a faint green line all the way up to his mind. "He . . . the killer meant to kill him, but the killer hasn't killed before. Angry, and deliberate, and scared of what he was doing. But he felt compelled. He had to do it. He had to. If it was a he. I don't know. I think he tried to hold him under the water, and when that didn't work and the victim started struggling, he pushed the cooler in. The victim was too slow to get out before . . ."

A question I couldn't quite hear. Something about evidence Freeman could corroborate.

"Give me a second," I said, and moved around the space again. To the right, the smooth pull of swimmers swimming laps, over and over, repetitive forever. Beyond the wall into the next apartment, a long-standing marital quarrel repeated until it sunk into the distant walls. The thoughts of the police, ordered and irritated at delays, newest and most fleeting, up in the shallows.

But above and drowning out everything else within reach, that fear. That fear would live in this place, over that hot tub, for a long time. Mindspace held onto emotions for days, sometimes, but I thought it might hold on to this fear for weeks, maybe longer.

I surfaced slowly, attempting to shake off that terrible fear. I shook it off, finally, as I left Mindspace behind, and opened my eyes, feeling smaller and infinitely more vulnerable. The victim had been so, so afraid in the end.

I saw Freeman was already motioning for the crime scene techs to come in and vacuum up the water for better photos of the body. They'd process the water, later, for evidence, but they didn't need me for that.

I knew what had happened. I knew it. But I couldn't prove it, and I was nearly out of time for the day.

"Tell me what's going on," Freeman said, after he'd pulled me over to the side of the scene near the tiled wall while the crime scene techs started the vacuum cleaner for the water.

"You were thinking this was an accident, right?" I started.

He nodded. With the journalist having published several

articles lambasting police corruption, though, he'd make sure every forensic *i* was dotted and *t* was crossed. Even if the man was just an alcoholic.

I winced at that one, internally, literally having to bite my tongue to keep from commenting. I'd been an addict once. This guy had done some things . . . some really important things, journalist-wise. He wasn't "just" an addict any more than I was. Even if, in the hot tub, he'd been stupid and irresponsible.

"Spit it out," Freeman said. "We are on the clock here."

I shook my head and pushed my anger aside. "He was afraid. Not the kind of panic you feel when you've drifted under the water after drinking—not a quiet biological wind-down while drunk. Trust me, he saw his death coming, and he was afraid of somebody killing him. No way this was an accident."

"Hmm," Freeman said. "You said that before. Is there any physical proof?"

"I assume you're going to do an autopsy," I said.

He nodded.

"Look for perimortem bruising around the neck and shoulders," I said. "That wouldn't be there if he drowned from the alcohol alone, and I had a strong impression of pressure on him, and struggle. There was no way this was an accident," I said again, some of the anger leaking into my voice. We needed to take this seriously. Alcoholic or not, stupid or not, this guy had been murdered. He deserved justice.

"I heard you," Freeman said. "He had at least four drinks though, judging from the scene. Could it have been a hallucination?"

I took a breath. It was a fair question, and deserved a fair answer. "Neighbor said he was a drinker. His tolerance was likely pretty high. I don't know. I don't think so, not at that stage. He felt with it, just slow."

He made a noncommittal noise. "Did you get a time of death?"

I reached out, sampled Mindspace again, to get a feel for how quickly my own mental signature was fading from the space, and compared it to the older ghosts of emotion. Then I looked at my cheap watch and counted backwards. "I'd say about eleven o'clock, maybe a little later. Mindspace tends to fade in a predictable pattern, and that seems about right for the fade level."

"Eleven, eleven-thirty last night then," he said, and nodded. Then he looked at his own watch. "You're here for another half hour?"

I nodded.

"Why don't you go fill out a written report with the scene officer then. I'll see you tomorrow when you come in again, assuming Branen assigns you back to this case."

"Why wouldn't he?"

He grunted. "Murder case priorities constantly shift. Until the ME report comes back with bruising or whatever else, this one still looks like an accident. Plus he's an alcoholic drowned in the hot tub. Except for the journalist angle, this one is an open-and-shut. There will be higher priority cases."

"It's not an accident!" I barked at him. "I'm telling you it's not an accident!"

"Yes, but can you prove it?" Freeman asked me evenly. I could feel his irritation.

"He deserves justice just like every-damn-body else," I said. By this point, Cherabino would have taken my word at face value.

Freeman just looked at me. "Anything else you need to tell me?"

"No." Other than the fact that he shouldn't just dismiss a victim like this. Especially somebody who'd made a career out of exposing wrongdoing. He'd saved hundreds of kids from those sweatshops. That had to matter, right? And exposing corruption and worse? Drugs or no, alcohol or no, that had to matter. "No, I guess," I said, but I was pissed and sure he could tell.

"Then go fill out the report. We'll need to make sure all our details line up for this one if it gets back-burnered. In case we need to pick it back up."

"Fine." I did what I was told, but there was no way this one was getting dropped. No way.

Freeman was just being an ass.

That night, I brought Mexican food back to the PI office. Mine, two bean and tofu burritos with every conceivable topping known to man. For Cherabino, a plain soy-chicken quesadilla, with a capped side of salsa in case she felt adventurous. It was cold outside in February, but I'd wrapped the takeout boxes in a blanket from my locker at the department to keep them warm inside the bag while I'd walked

I turned on the overhead light when I came in the front door. The industrial lights popped, turning on in a line from the empty reception desk to the back office area to the closed-off bathroom all the way in the back. The large picture-windows—the bane of our heating bills this time of year—turned reflective with the now-brighter light. Cherabino sat behind her desk, staring at paperwork under a small office lamp, having apparently not moved in hours.

I walked over to her, pulling out her box of food from the bag. "I have food," I said. I was still frustrated over Freeman and everybody else's dismissive attitude, but I'd been paid a paycheck by the department and we could actually afford takeout.

She looked up at me, exhaustion in every line of her body. "Leave it on the desk," she said, and went back to her reference book and paperwork.

Now I was pissed. I put the food on the corner though, and waited. I even put a bamboo-disposable fork on the top. Then I waited some more. My own food was getting cold.

"What is it, Adam?" she finally asked me. She was cold, cold as the Great White North.

"You're not okay, are you?"

"I'm fine," she said. She put her pen down then, and like it was a chore, pulled the food towards her. She opened the top, saw it was a quesadilla, and was visibly disappointed. "Thanks for bringing me something." Her tone was unconvincing.

"If you want to talk about it…," I started, cautiously.

She glanced up, then down again. "I'm fine, Adam, really. I've got some work to do for a new client, okay?" She took a determined bite of the quesadilla.

"Who's the new client?"

"Just some guy who wants me to do some research for him. It's not a big thing. You've got your own case to work now, don't you?"

I looked at her.

She looked at me.

"Yeah," I said, and took my own food to my desk. I forced it down, tasting only ash.

The next morning I arrived at the department bright and early. Michael Hwang was walking up the wide stone front steps right when I arrived. I could feel his attention grab onto me as he noticed I was there—like the feeling you get when someone is looking at you across a crowded room, hard to ignore.

I turned around. "Michael," I said.

He paused, foot on the step, discomfort radiating from him. Finally he said, "How is she?"

Cherabino had been a homicide detective—and Michael's boss—until her firing from the force for police brutality charges. Those charges were unjust, but Michael didn't know that, and it wasn't my place to tell him.

"She's okay," I told him, not knowing what else to say.

He put his hands in his coat pockets, his breath fogging in the February air. "Is . . ." he trailed off.

I was a telepath, and he was thinking very loudly, in a stop-and-start tug-of-war between his loyalty to Cherabino and care for her as a person and his utter contempt for brutality. If it were anyone else, he would have distanced himself long ago. He might still..

"She's settling into the private investigation agency with me," I said, the part I knew was fine for public consumption. "She's adjusting. The stress level might be better for her there." If we could ever make any money, that was.

Michael met my eyes, frowned, and then looked away. "Well, good." He started climbing the stairs again, moving on in more ways than one.

I took the door he held open for me—courteous to a fault, was Michael—and knew that he wouldn't be calling her, or me, any time soon.

I sighed and moved on, further into the department building where I had work to do. Work that might be the only money we had coming in right now. Well, except for Cherabino's mystery client.

Freeman found me in the coffee closet, where I was doctoring a cup of bad coffee and considering a very stale donut.

"Ward," he barked, from just outside the door.

"Yes?" I stuck my head out into the hallway.

"Come here for a moment please," he said. Another detective was walking away, clearly leaving a conversation with him.

I went back, grabbed the hard-as-a-rock donut, and then went back to Freeman. "What's going on?" I asked him.

His face was scowling at me—but it might just have been the scar, because his mind was calm, ordered, working on a problem. "The medical examiner's report came back on the Jeffries case, and you might be right."

"Excuse me?"

"I said you were right. There was some evidence of weak manual strangulation on the victim, bruises mostly, though the cause of death was most likely arrhythmia. The victim's blood alcohol level was a 1.2, a bit over the legal limit for intoxication, but the ME says there's not enough water in the lungs to indicate drowning. That's the trouble though."

"His head was underwater," I said, after a glance around to make sure we wouldn't be heard out of context. Not that it should have mattered in a police station, but even so. "No wait, the witness found him with his head out, and then it got moved by Jamal with the cord. Wouldn't he get water in the lungs at that point?"

"The ME says sometimes electrocution seizes muscles. The throat muscles were forced closed, which I suppose could have suffocated him. ME says there's no way to be sure. No signs of vomit, though, which is the more typical method of death in an alcoholic, though usually it's at a higher BAC."

Ha. I was right. "So it wasn't an accident."

Freeman shook his head. "ME says bruising isn't conclusive. Neither is the device we found—old cooler, apparently, with a nonfunctional safety switch. Intentional or accidental, impossible to say. And this guy was an alcoholic. I mean, there's not a lot of reason to go much further than this one. We interview the wife, and we move on."

"Hold on a minute," I said. "We have a legitimate victim. We get justice for the victims. That's what we do."

"He was an alcoholic. You know how that is."

"No," I said. "No, I really don't. Being an addict doesn't necessarily make you a bad person. He's a journalist. He's doing good work. Useful work! You can't just walk away on this one. It's not fair."

He took a moment to digest that, but chose not to comment on it. Instead he said, "Time of death was about midnight, the ME said. You weren't far off."

I took a bite out of the donut more out of habit than anything else, and made a face at its staleness. I chewed the dry thing anyway, to buy myself time to calm down, and swallowed, like swallowing sawdust. "I still say it was earlier, but whatever. Accidental is still an option, you're saying? And with the water that way, there's no way they can get prints from the neck."

"Right."

"Look, all I'm saying is, this guy deserves justice as much as anybody else. And what about his work? Wouldn't it look bad to his fellow reporters if we just dropped the case, get us in even more trouble? This kind of politics says to me we need more time solving this one, not less." I was angry. Very angry, at the dismissive attitude now even Freeman was having. Did people think this way about me? Did my work not matter because of things I'd done in the past?

Freeman paused. "There's political pressure to drop this one quickly. Branen wants it gone. And it could be an accident. Legitimately. It could be an accident."

I stared at him.

His face twisted again, around the scar, his mind

thoughtful. "The politics still don't help. But maybe you're not so wrong. I have some rope on this one. But it's tricky."

"Tricky?" I prompted, but my tone wasn't friendly.

He'd been talked to twice today by department brass, his mind said. This morning. Already. "The brass thinks we'll come out looking like a fool if we get too deep into this one. If we go through his old cases, his notes, and we find something against the department, it's on public record."

"So?"

Freeman's face twisted a little around the scar; his mind was . . . thoughtful. "Look it up. He's the anti-corruption reporter lately. Caught a politician, two Decatur city officials, and no less than four beat cops from the county taking bribes. Sometimes worse."

"What do you mean by worse, exactly?"

"Do your homework," he said, and even his mind didn't give me much more. "We've got the wife waiting for you in the interview room. I'd like to get her excluded or read in today. Then we'll see."

"Not a problem about the wife," I said. "Listen, I don't like this one being swept under the rug." The more they said *alcoholic* and *doesn't matter*, the more I wanted it to matter.

He paused. "I'd prefer to finish what I start, given the choice. But it's a political football. They say to drop it, you're usually better off dropping it."

"You chickening out?" I asked.

"I don't chicken out," he said, and walked away.

I looked after him, not exactly sure what he wasn't saying. There was subtext there, I knew, and it bothered me that I didn't know what.

Reading minds gave you more information, but it by no means made you understand.

One thing I knew, though: Jeffries had to get justice. Right? He had to, just like everybody else. Otherwise, why did I get up this morning and come in here? Justice had to matter. It had to.

Even for alcoholics and addicts. Even if they didn't deserve it.

I moved into the interview room—the first and nicest one—with a smooth gait, opening the door and closing it behind me gently. O'Hare, a younger cop I barely knew, was babysitting in the corner and nodded to me when I walked in. He'd already brought the suspect coffee, and from the delicious smell, it wasn't sim coffee, but someone's private stash.

I forced a smile, which always felt awkward but I could usually pull it off, and greeted the suspect. "Mrs. Jeffries . . ."

"Patricia. And the last name's Arnold, actually. I kept my name." Patricia was a plain thirty-something stocky woman, short at maybe five-two, with frizzy blonde hair, a crooked nose, and deep lines around her eyes. She was wearing scrubs, no makeup, and seemed tired. She also had a tension about her, a low-level worry combined with something else . . . something I couldn't quite name. Combined with Freeman's hidden meanings, I felt behind.

But I had to do my job, and today's tactic was honey instead of vinegar. I forced a smile again. "Patricia. Thank you

33

for coming down to the station so we could use our files here. I know the basement isn't the friendliest of places."

"It's dirty," she said, almost an add-on from my comment. "Heads would roll at the hospital if we let things get to this point."

I considered defending the department's honor, but honestly, they let it get dirty with full intention. Supposedly it increased the rates of confession; I didn't know. "You work at the hospital?" I asked her.

She nodded. "DeKalb General. In the mother and baby ward. Labor," she explained, when I looked blank. "It's one of the smaller hospitals for labor right now in the area, so there are only six of us nurses to cover the floor. I love it. There's nothing like seeing new life coming into the world."

I nodded and made a note not to ask questions about her actual duties. "Were you working last night?" I asked.

"No, I'm going in after this." I caught a stray thought that she might have to change the scrubs before going in, because of the dirt.

"You seem tired," I said. It was odd she was going in after her husband was just found dead, but not suspiciously odd. Some people clung to normal routines.

"I'm not sleeping well." She looked at me. I looked at her.

"Since the death?" I asked.

She nodded, but didn't engage.

I looked down at the file. "It says here that you were at work on Sunday night from midnight to one a.m.?" Very soon after the time the ME—and my Mindspace estimate—had placed the victim's death to occur.

"That's right," she said, and I got a burst of almost-pride through Mindspace.

"Anyone see you there?" I asked.

"The mother I was called in for, Mrs. White, and her husband. The obstetrician—Dr. Jones—and the other nurses." She gave me two other names. "I was called in at the last minute when the mother went into labor a little before midnight."

"We'll check on that," I said, but she didn't blink when I said it, and I had no doubt that her story would check out. If it did, according to the ME's timeline, she had a nearly unbreakable alibi and couldn't have done the crime. I'd have to look up how long it took to get to the hospital from her apartment, but even I didn't think she could have been called in during the murder of her husband and still been able to make it to work on time. Even if she'd had the extra half-hour my estimate had given her.

"Tell me about your husband," I said.

"He was a reporter. He worked a lot of hours, and he made a lot of enemies," she said. "The latest article got him a death threat. He was very happy about that; it meant he was coming back as a reporter, he said. Back to his glory days. He was obsessed with those." She frowned. I got a stray thought that he'd been drinking heavier than usual lately, and been meaner. If it hadn't been for his money, she'd have left long ago.

It took an actual effort not to pursue the thought instead of what she'd said out loud. But I'd play by the rules for now. Death threats were worth asking about regardless. "A death threat? From who?"

"I don't know." I got a tinge of frustration, then, instead of the grief I was expecting.

"Are you and your husband having problems?" I asked, gently. She was hiding something.

I felt her make the decision to lie, and I held out a hand.

"Please don't lie to me, Patricia," I said, and played my trump card. "I'm a Level Eight Guild-trained telepath, and I'm not here for anything but the truth."

She blinked and sat back, and for the first time I felt a wave of fear. I could feel the thoughts swirling around her head like a mobile on cartoonishly high speeds. "I . . ." she started, then backed up to choose her words carefully. Finally she met my eyes. "Yes," she said. "Isaiah and I were having problems, yes. He yelled at me and he worked all the time, and he didn't respect my job. He said I didn't have to work. He didn't get it—he didn't understand why I wanted to work at the hospital. He didn't understand me at all. We fought, a lot. And he drank. He drank way too much. I can't say that I'm sad that he's gone."

"Did you think about counseling?" I asked, generally a safe question that would give me a lot more information if she explained the decision one way or the other.

"No," she said, then "No" again, more firmly. I felt tinges of regret and determination, both related to the no.

Here we went. "You're having an affair," I guessed.

She nodded, slowly, warily.

"Did Isaiah know?" I asked her.

"He did," she said. "He didn't care." The last was said with an almost palpable contempt.

"Oh." I waited a few beats more, and then asked, carefully, "How were you planning to leave him?"

"I wasn't. His family had money. I had money married to him. There wasn't any point." She shook her head. "I don't want to talk about this anymore."

I could have pushed. In other circumstances, I would have pushed. But if her husband really had known—and it seemed like she was telling the truth—that invalidated most of her motive and her lover's, whoever that was. Plus she had that alibi. Even if she had the motive somehow, perhaps with the money, she hadn't had the opportunity, or much of one.

I pulled out the pad of paper at the bottom of the stack of files and gave it to her along with a pen. "Write down the names and numbers of the nurses who were there at the hospital the night in question. We'll be following up with them soon."

"I didn't go into this to find another lover," she told me. "It's not like that."

Despite her apparent honestly, there was just something about her that felt off to me. Well beyond the cheating. I didn't have a lot of sympathy for her, despite her husband being just killed, and I usually had a lot of sympathy for families. I sighed. "Just write the information down, please."

A flash of anger went out into the room then. "You don't believe me," she accused.

"It doesn't matter what I believe," I said, and made a mental note to do a background check on her at some point. I hadn't gotten a good read on her in the interview, with her playing her cards very close to her chest, and that bothered me.

Something was niggling at me from the interview with the wife, some detail I couldn't quite put my finger on. I was hungry, but I wanted to talk to Branen about what Freeman had said before I ate. I hated the idea that they were pushing us to drop this case, and I just wasn't willing to do it. Branen would have to get an earful first.

The victim was an alcoholic, okay. And he was having trouble with his wife, and screamed at her. But he still mattered, didn't he? Those kids he'd saved years ago mattered. Even taking down corrupt cops mattered, if what Freeman was saying was right. How else was the department to keep the trust of the community, to get justice, except by staying on the straight and narrow? They should be giving the man a medal, not sweeping his life under the rug and saying *alcoholic* like it dismissed him, even if he'd done some really bad things. He still deserved justice. Some things mattered even if he was an alcoholic. They had to.

I waited in the line outside Branen's office on the third floor. Actually, the line looked like it was for his assistant's desk, in front of the closed office door.

I waited while a detective got told to come back later and the pool secretary from downstairs chatted with the assistant for about ten minutes about some scheduling matter. Only a few cops walked by, since we were on the top floor for administrators and brass, but all that did gave me extra room.

Then it was my turn. I was frustrated, but I was holding it in.

Branan's assistant, Kalb, was in his early thirties at most, thin with a whipcord strength, and the kind of dark hair and sharp features that I associated with a Middle Eastern heritage. He seemed easily distracted, looking up every time someone went by, and his clothes seemed a little too nice for the job and the department salaries. Maybe he just liked looking nice, I told myself. Just because I interviewed a lot of suspects didn't mean everyone was one.

"I'm here to talk to Branen about an ongoing case he assigned me to," I said. "I had a couple questions."

Kalb shook his head. "Sorry, he's dealing with a high-level brass issue right now. Isn't to be disturbed until at least tomorrow. I can take a message? Or give suggestions?"

I didn't want to wait, but, on the other hand, Branen being busy might keep me on the case longer by default. "I just had a question about the last case he'd assigned me to. The detective I'm working for had some questions about it and politics. Seems to think we should half-ass it."

Kalb smiled what seemed like a forced expression, par for the job. "Branen doesn't assign people to things without thinking about it, especially when there's politics involved. If he gave you the assignment, he had a good reason, and unless he changes his mind and tells you about it, it's probably safe to continue in the direction you've been going. Doing a good job is always the right answer."

That was a very common sense reply, and mollified me. Maybe Branen did want the case solved.

Kalb asked, "Listen, aren't you the telepath who's working for the department? Is it true you can read every stray thought

I have?"

I blinked. His feeling was . . . interested. Almost too interested, like he was one of the department gossips. But I also didn't quite mesh with his mind, so I didn't get more than a general impression and wouldn't, likely, without a lot of effort that I didn't feel like expending. "Most people are nervous around telepaths," I said. "Aren't you afraid I'll read your secrets?"

He laughed, but it was a nervous sound, with a nervousness that washed over him too. But that quickly changed back to gossipy interest. "So that's a yes? I bet you've heard a lot of things!"

"Nothing that I'm willing to talk about," I said, uncomfortable. "Tell Branen that I stopped by, okay?"

Reluctantly, he went back to professionalism. "Sure. I'll make a note of your visit now. Anything special you wanted to add?"

"No, just tell him I checked in."

"Will do."

I wandered across the second floor detective pool, ignoring the long gauntlet of hostile cops. These men and women hadn't trusted me to start with, since I was a telepath. Now they disliked me even more for being associated with someone who'd been fired on brutality charges. I walked through the cubicle maze while shielding against the waves of hostility until my head nearly pounded with the effort. I pushed through the hallway between the cubicles, eyes narrowed, until finally the space between the cubicles opened up some and I was on safer ground.

Michael had Cherabino's old cubicle. Andrew, Cherabino's old cubicle neighbor and forensic accountant, waved to me as I passed. I stopped, said hello, and took some of the Jamaican Blue coffee he offered me. As usual, it tasted amazing and made the area smell even better.

Michael was seated in the middle of Cherabino's old cubicle, and I stopped to stare, forgetting even to sip the coffee. The place was perfectly neat, nothing on the floor, nothing piled on the sides of the space, only a single vertical file folder holder on the desk next to him and a three-ring binder in front of him he was busy updating with new pages as he wrote a report in block caps on a gray-and-white form.

I cleared my throat, and he turned around. "Adam," he said, after a moment. "What can I do for you?" he asked, but his voice was more cautious than cheerful.

I had thought about catching up, about seeing how he and his wife were doing, asking about his existing cases, being friendly. We'd worked together a while. But, judging from his demeanor, the friendly portion—however long it had been there at all—was over.

I finally settled for asking, "How do I look up old newspaper articles? Can I do that in the department?"

Michael frowned, apparently not having expected that question. "What paper?"

"Atlanta Journal," I said.

"Depends. If they're connected to a case, they'll have them in Records, on the first basement level. But the library will have them all, on microfiche and cards, already indexed. If you need more than one and you want something specific, that would probably be faster."

I blinked. I hadn't thought of that. "Thanks."

"No problem." He waited for a long, awkward moment, and when I didn't say anything else, turned back around to work on more paperwork.

I tried not to take it personally. Tried very, very hard.

Things had obviously changed, and changed a lot, and it wasn't strictly my fault. But I had to deal with the aftermath anyway, and it really did feel damn personal.

The Decatur Library was a tall stone building from before the Tech Wars, old and faded, boxy and yet somehow regal, with a large concrete parking deck on the back like the tail of some preening bird. A small fountain stood out front, cluttered with leaves despite the mid-winter cold, but still burbling determinedly. I climbed up the front walk and opened the central door.

A long counter greeted me, with a cranky woman behind it whose mind radiated literal waves of irritation.

I told her what I wanted, and she pointed me in the direction of the back. There sat the periodical card catalog and the huge old humming microfiche machine, its fluorescent light putting out a low-level hum when I turned it on. This was an inconvenient way to do my homework on the case, but not the worst I'd experienced; I could do it. Since the end of the Tech Wars, computers were largely illegal, and terrifying; a madman had used them to destroy the world—along with computer implants in peoples' heads, smart houses, smart cars—and the world remembered. Bioengineering was fine, good even; medicine had advanced to a high level and we were all happy. But computers? Well, there were a few at the department, under heavy lock and key, but those who used them did so with distrust and three different layers of background checks. Sneaking in to use those computers without Cherabino was asking for trouble—no matter how much faster I could have gotten the information. So the cards and the microfiche would serve my purpose here.

Michael had been right; all I had to do was flip through heavy cards fluttering like leaves beneath my hands. Every article Jeffries had ever written for the Journal was there, referenced by name and date. The word *corruption* appeared in title after title. I looked up as another researcher, probably a student by the age, moved past me to find her own cards.

She was one of the few people I'd seen so far; the library was mostly deserted today. I noted the articles I wanted and went to find the microfiche for the machine I'd warmed up. The system was clunkier than the Guild's, more spread out, with larger typed cards and more content everywhere, but I'd been a professor once and I could handle a little research, even if I had to do it all by hand.

I set everything up, the low-level humming of the light bothersome but not debilitating; I'd trained with far worse as a telepath and still kept my cool, though that had been a long, long time ago, long before I'd fallen off the wagon and gotten thrown out of the Guild. The light was still irritating, but for now I could manage.

I started reading. I'd pulled the older articles first, the ones from twelve years ago—had it really been that long? Three hundred kids he'd gotten out of the sweatshops. Follow-ups with the kids in foster care two years later. Exposing shady political deals. Then nothing, or piddly neighborhood stuff, for years. Then a year ago, he made a comeback. *Police corruption!*, the first article proclaimed. Then it started giving specifics on a patrol officer who'd been caught taking bribes and, in a *Journal*-exclusive story, assaulting a street-level prostitute when she wouldn't give up information about one of her clients. The woman ended up in the hospital, her cheek and her livelihood broken, and there had been no less than two witnesses who came forward pointing at the officer—Will Washington, Sr.—as the unprovoked attacker.

A cynical part of me wondered about those witnesses. One had surfaced against Cherabino, after all, and she'd been set up. But somebody, somewhere had to be telling the truth, right? If he'd really hit the prostitute to make her talk, he deserved to be called up for it. And surely a journalist would know the difference.

It got worse. Three police officers were found selling drugs stolen from police lockup. A politician had been caught on a slightly-illegal public recording saying that he'd pressured a judge to drop the charges against the cops in question. And four more instances of police accepting bribes. Jeffries had found them all, called them all out.

I noticed then that all of the officers implicated worked for the department I worked for part-time. All of them. And more than half worked specifically for Lieutenant Branen, in the Robbery part of his department.

A chill went down my spine.

This is why they wanted to cover it up, wasn't it? They thought that somebody at the department had killed Jeffries. Or, just because Jeffries had made himself an enemy, when he'd gotten himself murdered they used the word "alcoholic" and looked the other way. Doing nothing.

That couldn't happen.

I found Freeman behind the department, on the porch where I usually went to smoke. It was quiet back there, for all it was cold with an icy wind.

A man was there with him, in plainclothes, his shoulders hunched forward, a man I was betting was a cop by the body language and level of comfort here at the station. He and Freeman both looked up as the door closed behind me with a bang. They went completely silent, which made me suspicious.

"Am I interrupting?" I asked, queasy. Wondering if Freeman was involved in any of what Jeffries reported.

"Why don't you come over here, Ward," Freeman said. "I'd appreciate your insight." The last, I thought, based on his mental mood, meant that I was supposed to observe telepathically and figure out if the guy was lying.

I walked over, keeping my shoulders low, my body language unprepossessing.

"This is Detective Washington," Freeman said. "He's on administrative leave until Tuesday because of his involvement in an incident with a prostitute and a bribery charge."

"Which hasn't been proven," Washington said, quickly.

I wondered what Freeman was doing talking to a guy like this.. But mostly I was pissed at Washington, if he really was one of the guys who'd been caught in corruption. That stuff was despicable.

"Which hasn't been proven," Freeman agreed. "Internal Affairs has the hearing on Tuesday, and Washington came in to talk to the union lawyer. He's agreed to talk to me, no paperwork, nothing on the record, to help me understand his relationship with Jeffries."

"Damn reporter," Washington said, almost spitting it, and followed it up with a string of curses under his breath.

Ah. Washington had been connected to the Jeffries case, past just the article. Now I knew why I was here. "Did you—"

Freeman cut me off with a shake of the head, indicating with a hand I was to stand next to him.

I went, brow wrinkling, angry, but willing to play along.

"I'm not asking you to talk about what happened with Ms. Cane," Freeman said, in an even voice. "Like I said, I'm looking into the death of the reporter. Some have suggested . . ." Freeman shrugged, as if to dismiss the suggestions, "that you have motive to have killed him, since his accusations are what started your problems in the department." Ah, there it was.

"You mean when I was suspended?" Washington spat out. He was thinking he'd probably lose his job, and he needed this job. And then a lot of invective against both the prostitute and Jeffries. He was sounding more like a suspect all the time.

"Yes, that's what I mean," Freeman said evenly. "He had wronged you, and it's not a secret that you can take it personally when people do that. Strictly off the record, did you take it personally this time?"

"You better believe I took it personal," Washington said. "But I didn't kill the guy. Maybe I had motive—I mean, sure, I had reason to hate him—but I didn't kill him, no matter how much I wanted to." I got a picture of him yelling at the reporter, and the general feeling of anger, truthfulness, and regret at missing his chance to hurt the man.

Freeman glanced at me. Taking his cue, I nodded.

Then I looked at Washington. "Did you meet Jeffries face to face?"

"Well, yeah," the man said. "I went over to his apartment that day and told him if he didn't stay out of the thing with Internal Affairs I'd kill him. He'd done enough damage already, and he'd been talking about sending over his notes to be read into evidence. I wanted to beat him the hell up, but my lawyer said that sort of thing would get me fired for sure, just one bruise he said, so I spat on the floor next to him and I left."

Freeman was staring at me. I paused. There was a great deal of truth in Washington's statement, it felt like, but he was lying, at least on the fringes, at least to himself.

"Really," Washington said into the silence, now directly at me. "Really, man. You're here to read the truth, right? You're a telepath, right? I'm telling you the truth now. I didn't kill him. I wanted to, but I wasn't anywhere close to there. I was at home, watching threedee programs. I . . ." he trailed off, shook his head in anger.

"He is telling the truth," I told Freeman. *Mostly,* I added, mind-to-mind. *The strict letter of what he's saying is true. I can't tell you further than that.*

"What time were you at Jeffries's apartment?" Freeman asked, his voice unchanging from the neutrality he'd used thus far.

"I don't know, maybe four o'clock? It was afternoon, before rush hour. Couldn't have been later than that. Listen, can I go? I've got to meet with the union lawyer today, and he's not going to wait for me forever."

"I have one more question," I said, thinking back to the autopsy information Freeman had shared earlier. "It's not a big deal either way, but I need to account for some bruising. Did you put your hand around Jeffries's throat?" I held up a hand at his protest. "He clearly didn't die from it, and I'm not judging, but I need to know."

Intense rage came from Washington then, rage intense enough I well believed he could kill, given the right moment and opportunity.

Freeman put his hand on the man's shoulder. Quietly, he said, "It won't go anywhere. Like the man said, we need to account for bruising. Yes or no, that's all we need."

The anger cooled a little at Freeman's words, though Washington still glared at me with resentment.

"Yes or no," Freeman prompted again, so quiet you almost couldn't hear it.

Washington took a breath, then another. His anger still bubbled up, but more quietly. "I didn't kill him, I said. I didn't."

"We understand," Freeman said. "We do."

Washington looked down at him. "I didn't touch him. I threatened him, okay? I threatened him pretty good. But I didn't touch him. Wherever the bruises came from, it wasn't me."

And that last bit was the honest truth, no hedges, no exceptions, when it came to that particular incident in the afternoon. My gut said it was truth for the wider case, but I didn't know that, not really.

"Of course," Freeman told him, without changing his expression at all. "Thank you for helping me with my case. I wish you luck with the lawyer."

"Yeah. Don't bring any of this up with IA, okay? I've got it bad enough without getting me involved in Jeffries. Who I didn't kill."

"If your story checks out, I don't see a reason to mention it," Freeman told him.

Washington looked at me, significantly.

"I'm a telepath," I said after a second. "I can keep a secret." It didn't mean I *would* keep his secret, not if I was wrong and he'd killed somebody, but he didn't see that. They never did.

"Okay," he said, and left.

Freeman waited for a long moment, for the door to close behind Washington and him to walk far enough away. I shivered, settling a little deeper into my coat.

I was amazed. I knew that I wouldn't have gotten a tenth of the information from that guy—especially once he knew I was a telepath—that Freeman had gotten freely. Cherabino wouldn't have done much better than me. And calming him down to get an honest answer at the end—Freeman was good. Very good. And he was obviously investigating this case again, far beyond what he had to do.

"I thought you were going to drop this case," I said to him, finally. "I mean, didn't you say the department wanted you to drop this case?"

Freeman shifted his weight, looked out into the brown-grass courtyard. "Yeah, well. He is a victim, and you're right about the other reporters. Maybe it's worth a look. I'd rather finish what I started anyway."

"Even with the brass wanting you to drop it?" Maybe I'd misunderstood what was going on here.

That made him turn around to look me directly in the eye. "Nobody's given me an order yet. I've got options, I can use them. Where have you been, the last few hours?"

I took a breath. "Decatur Library, looking up newspaper articles. I have a list of people that Jeffries's articles hurt, at least the recent ones. Washington's on the list. So is a politician who was out of the country during the murder."

Freeman nodded, slowly, his scar pulling again unattractively as he thought. "We'll need to compare notes and make sure I haven't missed anyone. I've been working off the department's suspension lists." He'd talked to a dozen cops today, quietly and respectfully, like he had with Washington. Nobody else had nearly the motive that this guy did, and watching programs at home didn't equate to a real alibi. "We need to keep Washington on the short list of suspects," he said.

Once again I couldn't quite believe that Freeman was doing

this much, this quickly, when he'd been so against it earlier.

"Washington was telling the truth," I said. "Mostly, anyway." And Freeman had been surprisingly cordial to the man, very hail-fellow-well-met. "I thought you liked the guy." He'd certainly treated him well, with a real connection that had paid off in real information.

Freeman shrugged. "He's a fellow cop. Even if he's dirty as hell—and with the IA investigation, I don't see any reason to doubt it—he's a guy who's chosen to put his life on the line. That deserves respect as long as he has that badge."

"Oh," I said. I didn't know how to feel about that attitude. Wasn't there right and wrong, good and bad, when it came to people? Wasn't that what everybody had implied with all the alcoholic comments?

"Doesn't mean he's not guilty. Besides. You're the big shot interrogator here. Which tactic gives you more information, respect or intimidation?"

"Um . . ." Honestly, it depended on the subject.

"With fellow officers, it's respect, and I don't see any reason not to extend that respect to the citizenry, barring really serious crimes. Sometimes even then, if it gets you somewhere." He shook his head, like he was throwing off a bad feeling. "I need a cup of coffee now, and I'd like to see your research before you have to leave for the day and I need to move onto other cases."

"Okay," I said, and followed him back upstairs to his desk. "Well," I said in the elevator.

"What?"

"How deep do you think this thing in the department

goes?" I asked. He probably wasn't the one to ask—thin blue line and all that—but I couldn't keep the words from coming out.

Freeman shrugged, the ancient elevator moving infinitesimally upwards. "Hard to tell. You get one bad apple, you get another. IA is on it, though. They'll get to the bottom of it sooner than later. The department will survive."

That . . . was an odd way to put things. I still felt like an outsider, sometimes, and I wasn't concerned with the department surviving. I was concerned with the right thing, and with the citizenry getting the protection its tax dollars had paid for. I was concerned, like the journalist, with shutting down the corruption, not protecting the system.

"We've got plenty of work now," Freeman said. "We'll get to the end of our run of clues, we'll send any excess to IA, and we'll find the truth. Or we won't. But we'll do the job."

The elevator doors opened then, and he walked off.

Freeman was . . . different. A lot different than Cherabino, for all they worked the same job—or had. He worked less hours, I was betting, but he seemed . . . more direct. More clear on what he was doing and how to get to the end. But also, less idealistic. More about the cops. More about the in group and the out group.

I admired that clarity, maybe even preferred it. But the idealism . . . I missed that too. Cherabino wouldn't have sided with a dirty cop, even out of respect. At least I didn't think she would.

I felt like I was standing on sand. But Jeffries—any guy who did the right thing, who found the corrupt and made them pay, well.., he deserved justice. He did. Bad guy, rough on his wife, hitting the booze and all. He still deserved justice. Didn't he?

I spent the next hour going through records with Freeman and comparing notes, at his small cubicle towards the front of the detective floor. His neighbors noticed me when I walked up and then looked away. There were a lot fewer thoughts about me standing next to him, a lot less hostility, than there had been a year ago when I'd been on my own or working with Cherabino. Even a lot less than when I'd walked through the cubicles on my own earlier today. I resented that.

Freeman's cubicle was sparse, a few well-worn pictures of family on the walls, and his filing system was nothing more than three-ring binders in stacks—labeled yes, neat no. Some of the binders looked older than I was. He seemed . . . comfortable here. Not as scattered as Cherabino had been, not as prim and neat as Michael. Just comfortable, serviceable Freeman, who got the job done.

I walked him through my research, he walked me through the high-level results of the interviews for the day, some of which were off the books and so didn't have more than a few scribbled notes on a page in a binder. He kept names out of it, given that we were sitting in the open cubicle area, and kept the words to a sentence or two, knowing that I'd read his assessment off his mind anyway. Then he gave me a copy of the autopsy report, which I was settling down to read when we got interrupted.

A beat cop in uniform—an unusual sight on this, the second floor for detectives—cleared his throat at the entrance to Freeman's small cubicle. I looked up. He turned around.

"Yes?"

"Adam Ward?"

"Yes?" I said.

"You're listed as the emergency contact person on Isabella Cherabino's record for non-medical emergencies."

My heart sped up, and I put the papers down. "What's going on?"

"Could you come with me please?"

I grabbed my bag and followed him, very worried. I got even more worried on the elevator when he pressed the button for the first basement, the one that let out on the lower level behind the building, the level that held the holding cells.

"What did she do?" I asked him.

The beat cop squirmed a little. "She was found on site attempting to use her former credentials to look up a citizen's traffic record, including his address." The subtext was disapproving. Clearly, whoever this guy was, he was by-the-book.

I winced. "How long ago was this?" I could completely believe that Cherabino had tried to bend the rules to work on a minor case for the agency, but I found it hard to believe that I hadn't noticed her mind in the department. It had been a long day, but even so . . .

"She's been in there about three hours, while her former supervisor decided whether to press charges."

"Branen decided not to press charges?" I hoped. I guessed.

He nodded. "She's getting off with a warning *this time*, and it looks like the Records department was prompt in calling for help, so no privacy laws were compromised. Please emphasize to *Ms.* Cherabino that she cannot legally enter these premises again unless she is arrested."

"I will." I swallowed. She was going to be fit to be tied. And I still had to come back tomorrow morning and finish up this case. Could I leave her?

The ancient elevator hit its correct floor with a lurch I could feel in my bones. The doors opened, displaying a row of five cells on either side, plus a larger, wheelchair-accessible one at the back. Holding only; anyone who'd be locked up more than twenty-four hours got a berth across the street in jail. Even so, most of the cells were full, and by the smell of them, mostly with drunks.

Cherabino was in the third cell on the right, sitting curled up in the corner, utter defeat and anger on her face and in her mental signature. She looked up when we got in front of the cell, and she stood up, slowly, every line of her body angry.

"You're free to go, *Ms.* Cherabino," the beat cop said, and unlocked the door with a set of keys he'd had on his belt.

"Thank you," she said, through her teeth, meaning anything but.

A half hour later, as I settled into the passenger seat of her car and she put her things in the back seat. I could still feel her anger.

The driver's side door closed after her, and she gripped the steering wheel hard, her knuckles turning white with the pressure on the wheel. Her thoughts nearly freezing with the pressure on her mind.

"Are you sure you're safe to drive?" I asked her, evenly. I didn't usually drive but considering her usual recklessness and current mood, I would take over if I had to.

"Yes. No." She blew out a breath of air. Took in another. Visibly relaxed her hands on the wheel. "In a minute."

It was still cold outside, the February sun not nearly bright enough to make the inside of the car uncomfortable, even parked directly in that sun. So I'd wait.

"What happened back there?" I asked. "You know—"

"I don't want to talk about it," she spat, cutting me off.

"If it was for a client for the agency, you're going to have to talk to me eventually," I said.

After a moment, staring straight ahead, she said, "No. No, I won't. It won't happen again." Then she cranked the car up, the whine as the small fusion warmed saying everything she was willing to say.

No matter how I pushed her, she cut me off, walling me off. By the time she dropped me off at my apartment, I looked at her retreating car, caught between hurt and anger myself.

Sure, she'd lost a hell of a lot when she'd lost her job, but this was just stupid.

I went inside and called my Narcotics Anonymous sponsor. "I need a meeting," I said.

The next morning, I reported to Lieutenant Branen, the head of Robbery and Homicide, and my and Freeman's boss. I couldn't in good conscience not report in.

I knocked on his door. It was still twenty minutes before shift change, but he was there like I knew he'd be, head lowered over paperwork.

He looked up. "Ward. Come in and close the door." He set the paperwork aside and smiled his habitual empty smile.

I closed the door and sat uncomfortably in the guest chair. "I'm checking in again, since you assigned me to the Jeffries case with Freeman and I've already spent so many hours there. Is it true you give him more of the political ones than anybody else? Freeman seems to think that you want to just bury this case. Is that true?"

Branen frowned at me. "I wouldn't say that, officially. Freeman and his team are reliable, and they don't get intimidated by high profile cases. In this one, I didn't think we'd get away with anything but a thorough investigation. The *Atlanta Journal* will be all over it if we're seen to be shirking. But yes, I'd rather it turn out to be an accident and his investigations go away. That's not a secret."

"You'd rather it be an accident. And saying that loudly isn't going to prejudice the case at all."

Branen sat back in the chair and sighed. "For a man who spends most of the day in other peoples' heads, you're sure blunt this morning. I'm afraid we don't have the luxury of assuming accident in this kind of case, even if we'd like to, and I've talked to Freeman and heard his concerns. He'll follow it to the end. That doesn't mean you need to spend a lot more time there, especially since we're up against your time allotment for the month soon. I have another task for you today, actually." He seemed worried. He also didn't want me focusing on the Jeffries case, and I got the impression more than half of what he'd said was a lie.

I read a little deeper, risking him realizing I was in his head. Oh. Oh, the *bastard*! He'd assumed since I was an addict, I'd half-ass any job involving an addict and assume the guy had done the thing to himself. Self-hatred or some such. I pulled out of his head, angry.

I hadn't slept well, and it bothered me that he was lying to me, bothered me more that he'd just assumed I'd do a crappy job. I still needed this job, so I forced myself to ask, "What's the task?"

"My . . ." Branen trailed off, and moved forward again in his chair to a more normal position. "You remember Kalb? My assistant? He's been here almost a year now."

"Yeah," I said, not sure where this was going.

"Well, um. It's the unfortunate truth that when the technicians identified the fingerprints from the Jeffries apartment as part of their murder scene processing . . . my assistant's fingerprints were at the scene. As he wasn't part of the investigating team, I was notified. He's due into the office in a few minutes, and I'd like you to question him. Carefully. He's still a member of this department. But considering Jeffries's history of reporting on this department . . . well, we can't rule it out, and I need you to be thorough."

That made me blink. "You want me to question Kalb like a suspect?"

Branen nodded, slowly. I could feel both his regret and determination. "I'd sit in, but since he works so closely with me we need to have as much distance and impartiality as possible. *Please* make your report thorough, and file it on time this time. I'll give him a few days' administrative leave if he clears, but I'll need to know whether to pursue more by this afternoon. I'll pay for your overtime if it comes to that."

"Let me see if I get this right. You want me to decide whether your assistant is hiding enough to justify . . ." I trailed off. Maybe Branen did care about the corruption, about justice, just really differently than I did.

"To justify some kind of action by the department, possibly firing. Yes. And don't worry; you might not be able to testify in a formal court of law, but both Paulsen and I will stand for your character in the interview room if it comes to an internal investigation. You're one of the least political interrogators we have on the payroll, and that will only help this case." He looked pained. "I . . . can't help but think if I hired him . . ."

"Whatever he's done or not done, you couldn't have known," I said, feeling his mix of emotions: guilt, worry, determination, a sense of fairness, and self-recrimination. Only innocent people felt like that in the absence of clear information. It was odd; Branen had always seemed so strong, so in control, so much the boss I'd never before now thought of him as human. And I hadn't liked Kalb. But still. Maybe this was my answer, Branen doing something I could respect.

I added, "You're sure my relationship with Cherabino isn't going to be an issue if this does turn into an internal investigation? There are more interrogators here. She was just pulled into holding yesterday."

Branen sighed again, looking beat up. "I heard about that. I understand, she's a loose cannon right now, but you've done exceptional work the past weeks. I don't think we have an interrogator in the building who doesn't have some kind of bias. Your bias doesn't impact this one at all. You pursue it, we'll get it on tape, and we'll figure out what to do from there." He looked me in the eye then. "Tell me I can count on you, Ward."

"You can count on me," I said, and swallowed. He trusted me to do a good job here, where it was trickier, when he didn't before on a more usual case?

I left promptly when ordered, not sure how to handle any of this. Was this related to the bad apple thing Freeman was implying? Or was it a distraction to get me away from the Jeffries case?

Or was I just being paranoid?

I waited in the sound room of the third interview suite, staring at Kalb as he squirmed in the chair at the other side of the one-way glass. I wanted to smoke, but the tech wasn't okay with that, even with the industrial-strength filter on, and today I didn't feel like being more of an asshole than I had to be.

Kalb wore a pastel blue dress shirt and dark slacks of fine quality cloth, nothing I recognized, but clothes far too fine for the standard cop or detective's salary, not to mention the lower-paid position he filled as Branen's administrative assistant. Right now, here, that bothered me again. A shiny pin sat on his shirt front, a shape I didn't recognize but that probably meant something. He fidgeted nearly non-stop, first his hands against the table, then his foot bobbing against the floor, his body moving forward in the chair for a moment, then back, like he couldn't ever get comfortable. He was in his thirties but seemed younger, somehow. More uncertain.

After watching him for awhile and asking the technician a question, I settled on my approach for the day. I picked up a pile of files, more for something to do with my hands than anything else—I still wanted that cigarette between my fingers, badly—and ducked out into the hall and into the next room.

"Adam Ward," Kalb greeted as I walked in. "The telepath. It figures they'd send you." He seemed nervous, but at this stage, being questioned like a suspect, he'd be an idiot not to be nervous.

I paused at the door, glancing at the younger cop they'd sent to babysit me in the corner, somebody who—unlike me—could testify if and when this went to court. "Kalb," I finally said, channeling as much of Freeman's respect-between-equals as I could manage. It wasn't a comfortable approach. I sat down, putting the pile of files in front of me. Behind me, the babysitter shifted in his chair.

Then I did something I didn't often do: I sat there, quietly and calmly, and said nothing.

"They said you were going to ask me some questions about the Jeffries case," Kalb said into the silence after barely thirty seconds. "They came and got me at work. I was setting up a press conference for the lieutenant."

"I'm sure the lieutenant can take care of the details himself if it's critical," I said evenly, still channeling Freeman's calm as much as I could manage. It had worked for him with other members of the department, after all. "Jeffries was a reporter investigating corruption . . ." I started, letting the sentence trail off until it practically begged to be filled with something.

Kalb obliged, looking down at the table like he was ashamed, then back up, at me. "Look, I didn't know," he said.

"Of course you didn't know," I echoed, even changing some of my body language to echo his. I wanted his impulse to talk to be met with friendliness, to be met with someone very much like him, or so he'd feel. He was on the edge here, the edge of something big, and all I had to do was push him over it.

"That's what I'm saying!" Kalb said, and then stood up, running his fingers through his hair. "That's what I'm saying, but nobody would ever believe me."

"Which is why you didn't say anything then," I echoed, bringing the implication out loud. I couldn't get a clear read of anything but tortured emotions from him, but his body language was pretty clear. He wanted to talk. I just had to bring him to the right place.

"Exactly," Kalb said, and turned around, pacing a few times across the table, before sitting back down.

Beside me, the younger cop moved his hand away from his gun, quietly.

"Look, she didn't tell me she was married at first."

I blinked. That was not where I thought this was going, at all. To be honest, I'd thought he was gay, with the clothes and all. "Who?"

"Patricia, man. Patricia Arnold. Isaiah Jeffries's wife. The reporter. The reporter who's dead now." He looked at me like I was an idiot for not knowing.

Okay, now I was really confused. "Oh, of course," I said, empty words to keep him talking. "How could you know? They even had different last names."

"Exactly! And then she said her husband didn't care, and I didn't look into it too much, you know, because the sex was really really good and she was always taking me places and paying for things. She even bought me these clothes. And the sex was good. It was, okay? I didn't know then what she'd do with the information. She never told me her husband was a reporter. I mean, how was I supposed to know? I just thought, you know, she cared about my job and gossip and liked to laugh at people. And she always paid for things." He stopped, and backpedaled. "I didn't tell her anything she wouldn't have found out from anybody else who knew those guys. I mean, Washington was all over the rumor mill after that hooker thing happened, and Oswald, well, he's a prick, you know?"

But I had spent an hour talking to Freeman about the other people Jeffries had written up, so I knew who Oswald was. "You know he killed himself after IA started looking into the thefts from the lockup."

"That was sad. But he shouldn't have taken all those drugs and stuff at all, much less from police lockup. And the rest of the guys they found, well, that was a good thing, right? That kind of stuff. I mean, I didn't tell her anything she couldn't have found out otherwise and anybody doing bad stuff deserves what they get, I mean even the department has to feel that way."

"How did Lieutenant Branen feel about this?" I asked, having to work hard now at keeping my body language and face cordial and supportive. This guy had no business working with a police department or with any kind of confidential information. No business at all, I thought with contempt. Even if he had helped catch wrongdoers. What else had he shared?

Suddenly I caught myself in the thought—which was worse, the gossip who spilled secrets or the bad apple who took things for gain? It had to be the bad apple, right? But Kalb had been a whistleblower only by accident, and he'd broken ranks. Freeman would probably hate him for that. For me, I didn't know what to think. I believed in privacy and confidential information, but I also believed in real justice.

Kalb squirmed in his chair. "Well, I didn't fill out the relationship forms like I should have, and I feel bad for that. But I didn't know, okay? And by the time I did it was already in the papers and stuff. Branen would have been really mad."

He felt really guilty about something, and I needed to know what it was. "Did you kill Jeffries when you found out his wife was pumping you for information?"

"No!" Kalb yelled, and sat back, head in his hands. "No, it wasn't like that at all. I mean, she said he didn't care, that they were having problems and she couldn't leave because of the money. She kept buying me things, and she was fun, and it wasn't any of my business, you know? Until the stuff started showing up in the papers. That's when I said I couldn't talk anymore, but we could still go out. She seemed okay, but when I wouldn't tell her any more about the Commander—"

I cut him off. "Commander Draco?" The captain's boss, the administrative head of most of the county police force, a guy I'd never met and never wanted to—he was rumored to be pretty scary.

"Um," Kalb said, and for the first time his parade of words stopped cold.

I let the silence sit—for a minute, for two. Then I said, "What did you tell her about the Commander?"

Kalb was feeling guilty. Very guilty. "Look, I shouldn't have said anything. And I told Patricia that. I shouldn't have said anything at all. And I dug in my heels, and I didn't. I didn't tell her anything, even when she got really mad, I didn't, but that was when she said she had to stop seeing me. I mean, I pleaded with her, but she wouldn't. She said if I wasn't going to give her information anymore that her husband—Jeffries—would be really mad. Like, worse than hitting her mad. I told her she should get away from him, divorce him and stuff. I'd help her. But she laughed this ugly sound of a laugh and said the only way Jeffries would let her leave was if he was dead, and anyway there was the money and I'd served my purpose." He shivered. "That was really cruel of her. I'd served my purpose. But maybe she'll get away now, huh? With the money and everything. Now that Washington killed him. Maybe she'll call me again."

His story was like a fish darting around a large tank—impossible to pin down and more than a little hard to follow, if in this case well worth the catching for the strength of the information alone. It did sound like the wife had motive now. "What makes you think Washington killed him?"

Kalb stared at me. "That's what everybody's saying, right? Washington killed him because he got him in front of IA and probably fired."

Maybe, I thought. Maybe.

I'd always had good valence, good mental syncing, with Freeman, so I noticed him behind me on the other side of the one-way glass in the other room. He'd been hearing all of this, at least the last minute or so. And maybe he'd go after Washington right now. The man didn't have an alibi, at least not one we could confirm. But a couple of things were still bothering me.

"She said the only way she could get away from him is if he was dead?" I asked. "When was this?"

"The last time we talked, I mean, after the thing with the commander and before she stopped taking my calls. Maybe . . . maybe three weeks ago? Maybe four? She seemed really mad that day."

I leaned forward. "This is very important, Kalb. Very, very important, so I need you to be absolutely honest with me. Did she ever tell you she was going to kill Jeffries, or that she wanted him dead, other than that time?"

"Um, just the usual stuff," Kalb said uncomfortably, his shoulders hunching over. "I mean, everybody says they want their spouse dead, right? At least everybody screwing around, that's kind of the thing."

I sat back, feeling my suspicion crystallize. Maybe it wasn't the department. Maybe it was plain and simple—the spouse.

A knock on the door then, and Freeman's head poked in. "Can I come in?" he asked me.

"Why not."

"I'd like the chair," Freeman said evenly.

I stood, settling against the glass at the back of the room.

Freeman moved the chair slightly away from the table and sat down, heavily, his loose shirt settling like a cape around his body. His scar was still there, still prominent, but I knew through Mindspace he was more pensive than the judgmental crankiness his face implied. "Kalb, you're aware that as part of your job with the department you're entrusted with a variety of sensitive information, including and especially the information you come across as part of your job in assisting Lieutenant Branen?"

"Yeah." Kalb was squirming again.

"Let's talk about what you said about Commander Draco. What, exactly, did you tell this reporter's wife about one of the most powerful men in the department?"

"I didn't tell her anything criminal, I swear!" Kalb said, babbling anything and everything except what Freeman wanted to know.

"And how did you find out about this?" I asked. "How did you know before Internal Affairs knew?"

"People tell me things!" Kalb said. "People tell me things and they leave information just lying around, and sometimes they tell things to Branen even! There aren't any secrets, not really!"

"There aren't any secrets," I said, disbelievingly.

"No," he said.

Either Branen knew more than I'd had any idea, or Kalb was a better investigator than half the detectives in the building, with far more curiosity. I didn't know which answer I was more willing to deal with.

Freeman interrupted, "I'm here as an impartial investigator into the Jeffries case, and Adam here works for me. I'd like to find out what happened. Why don't you walk me through what you did say and what you didn't, and we'll figure this out."

Kalb took a breath, looking back and forth between Freeman sitting and me standing. And I got the first clear picture of what he'd said: based on several pieces of gossip together, Kalb was pretty sure Draco had been involved in the plot with the police who'd stolen from lockup. He'd asked for ten percent of the haul, according to Kalb's information. And Kalb wouldn't take much to tell Freeman all about it—he liked Freeman, and he wanted to talk about what had happened.

"I have another appointment," I lied then. "Detective Freeman will have to take over, but you're in good hands. He'll help you figure this out. Thank you, Detective."

"You're welcome," Freeman said without turning around.

As I left, I heard Kalb start to stutter through what he'd said about the commander. I got a stray feeling from him then—fear. Real, authentic fear of the commander, unmixed with respect or well-feeling. Fear of what the man would do when all of this came out. But his eagerness for gossip outweighed it all. No wonder he'd talked so much to his lover, if gossip drove him this much, if he went looking this much for dirt.

"You'll protect me from the commander, right?" Kalb asked Freeman.

I paused with my hand on the door.

"You'll have every chance to explain yourself through due process with Internal Affairs," Freeman said. "I think you'll find that the truth is the best policy. Tell me what's going on, and we'll figure it out together."

The fear eased the instant Freeman said the words "Internal Affairs," which was odd. I pushed through the door and moved into the room with the recording equipment.

Branen was counting on me to come to some kind of decision about Kalb. And, unless something very positive came out of the next few minutes, that decision wasn't going to be very good.

You didn't get to be a telepath and not have a strong sense of privacy and public versus sensitive information. Kalb had walked all over those kinds of ethics, without a second thought, his sense of justice and privacy fluid and self-serving. Worse, even when questioned about his actions, he still didn't think he'd done anything wrong.

But he had been part of what had brought corrupt cops to light and gotten them punished. He'd caught some people in wrongdoing, and effectively blew the whistle for a reporter, knowingly or unknowingly. And I'd worked with Cherabino too long, felt too strongly about justice and right and wrong, to feel comfortable with anything that covered up wrongdoing.

He'd done wrong, I thought, and I'd tell Branen that. But maybe—just maybe—his wrong had been the right thing in the end.

Now if I could just figure out where Jeffries fit into all of this, and whether his wife was involved in his death.

I stopped by Michael's cubicle, not knowing what else to do, and knocked on its side. A dull sound echoed from my imprint of knuckles to the fabric-covered material.

Michael looked up. His mind was wary. "Something I can do for you, Adam?"

"I need some advice," I said.

His face cleared a little then. "Sure, come on in." He pointed to a guest chair about two feet from him, a chair mysteriously cleared of debris. In Cherabino's old cubicle, that was a miracle all by itself.

I sat, cautiously. Not long ago I would have asked these sorts of questions of Cherabino or Bellury—his name hit me with a real pain, as I missed him, may he rest in peace. But Freeman was busy and not very chatty, and I wanted another perspective.

"Okay," I said, trying to figure out how to catch him up, before deciding to jump straight to the end. "I need to break the alibi of the wife of a murder victim. Based on her comments to some of the other parties—and a very strong motivation to get out of a bad marriage—my gut says it's her. But the ME's time of death is thirty minutes past mine from Mindspace, and by then she was called into her hospital with a last minute maternity case. Freeman's still stuck on another guy without a strong alibi, but I think the suspect is telling the truth. For once. The thing is, the victim wasn't a nice guy, and nobody seems to be all that interested in tracking down his killer."

Michael sat back a bit in the chair and thought. "Well, murder isn't illegal just for the nice victims. It's our job to find the killers either way. You think it's the wife? Have you talked to her coworkers? Confirmed her story?"

"I called and confirmed she was working that night," I said. "Her supervisor checked the records, and she came in at the time she said. The woman went into labor not long before that, the supervisor said. It checked out."

Michael thought. "You're sure it was her?"

"She was hiding something in the interview, and her husband and she were having trouble but she couldn't leave. She has motive."

"Well, just because the records say something doesn't mean it happened exactly that way. I'd go to the hospital and see if you can talk to one of her coworkers who was actually there that night. From the sound of it, fifteen minutes could make all the difference to your timeline."

"Twenty maybe, but yeah." I paused. Here was the part I really wanted another opinion on. "Do I need to take somebody with me? You know, since I can't testify?" My drug record was legally protected under the Second Chance Act, but any defense attorney in the world would destroy my credibility in ten minutes flat, so the department had been taking steps— like the babysitting cop in the interview room—for years. The question was, did I need one here? Michael was pretty good on the letter of the law and had been in court several times on Cherabino's cases. That and people liked people who asked them for advice. I'd like Michael to loosen up around me again if possible.

Michael thought. "Well, to show it in court you're going to want something. But this one's better with a witness anyway, I think. If your witness's credibility is good, it doesn't really matter who found her. You're on a timeline?"

I nodded. "I'm already at the end of my hours for the week, officially, and I'd like to get this done." Cherabino would probably want my help with her case at some point, and I was already over hours, but I really needed to see this to the end.

"You might just head on over then. See if something drops." Michael had been a beat cop for a long time, and he still had that sensibility. But in this case, he was probably right.

"I hate hospitals," I muttered.

"Why?"

I looked up. "People die in hospitals. Like, a lot of them. And there's pain and suffering, a lot of it, so that you walk in and you can't really feel anything else in Mindspace. It's painful."

"Sometimes I forget you're a telepath," Michael said.

"Um, thanks?"

"Not everything's easy, huh?"

"Not really," I said, and went to stand up.

"Listen, I've got heavy paperwork this week," Michael said. "You need more advice, I'll be around."

I smiled then, and it wasn't even fake. "That sounds great."

Labor and delivery at Decatur Hospital was a madhouse of pain, excitement, worry, love and fear. The emotions hit me in the face like a punch as soon as I walked over the line of the entrance. At least it wasn't the ER or anything—I'd walked all the way around the building to enter here, at the specific location, rather than chance a higher-traffic, higher-death area, which would be like a minefield in Mindspace.

I'd found the floor supervisor, who was irritated but finally let me talk to Ashley Watkins, a twenty-two-year-old nurse who'd been on shift the night in question. She had bleached-blond hair, too much makeup, a solid frame, and scrubs about a size too small. Also, bright green neon athletic shoes.

"Is there someplace we can talk quickly?" I asked her. "I'm looking into the death of Isaiah Jeffries, and I know his wife Patricia Arnold works here. It won't take long."

Her curious look cleared, and Ashley pulled me aside to a nook with a bunch of machines on carts, all turned off, fortunately. My telepathy didn't do well with large-scale electromagnetic fields. The rooms around me fairly vibrated with emotions, fear and pain and joy and everything, all mixed up into one, with a rhythm to it, a steady sure rhythm I found all too distracting if I let it in. So, as a result, with all the attention I had in keeping my mental shields up, I had very little to judge her truthfulness other than the evidence of my own eyes and ears.

"We only have a few minutes before I need to check Mrs. Manuel in 1247," she said. "What do you need to know?"

"You were on duty the night of murder, correct?" I said.

"That's right. I don't usually work Sundays, but they changed the schedule last week at the last minute, and I got moved from Wednesday to Sunday night. I was upset because I had a date I had to cancel pretty late."

"Okay," I said, and made a mental note to come back to that. "Tell me about Patricia. Do you know her well?"

"Well, she's not here right now if that's what you're asking. She seems okay. She's good with the patients, and she doesn't shirk her part. She doesn't let people get very close. So I don't know her very well. I don't think anybody here does."

"Is that unusual?" I asked her.

"Well, yeah," she said. "When you work this many hours with people, you get to be friends with most of them. At least that's what the others say. I've been here six months, and I know most everybody." She explained, "I got out of nursing school six months ago."

"Okay," I said. "So Patricia was here on Sunday night? Did you see her?"

"Yep, I saw her. Mrs. White went into labor that night, and she was on call, so she got called in. We had a full patient set already, you see."

"What time did you see her?" I asked.

"Maybe ten minutes before midnight? Yeah, that's about right. Mrs. White had been in active labor awhile by then, and I was having to juggle her and my other patients. I ran into her at maybe ten till at the shift station. She was updating the time logs. I fussed at her for being late—I'd called her in a little after eleven, and she'd known Mrs. White was probably going to pop that night. I mean, we all did. She'd come in that morning effaced at almost seventy percent, and she was already almost two weeks overdue."

I held up a hand to prevent her from describing medical things I really, really didn't want to know about. Then I actually thought about what she had said. "So Patricia was later than you thought she should be."

"Yes. Maybe a half hour. She doesn't live far from here, and like I said, it's not like she didn't know this one was coming."

"She was on call that night," I said. "And she'd had warning that she'd probably have to come in that night." I was starting to see that her famous last-minute alibi wasn't so puncture-proof after all.

"That's right," Ashley said.

"Did anybody see Patricia before you did?"

"I don't know of anybody. And anyway, she usually updates the logs right when she comes in so that's probably what happened that night anyway. We're all supposed to, but some of us do it at end of shift. She's a stickler for the beginning, though, since she keeps the schedule."

A big red flag went off in my head. "Let's back up," I said. "Patricia keeps the schedule?"

Ashley nodded and glanced at her watch.

"And your schedule got changed at the last minute to put you on duty on Sunday? Did Patricia's schedule get changed too?"

She looked over at the room at the end of the hall, seemingly itching to go already. "Oh, sure. She was supposed to be on call next week, not this week. But she said she had this big thing, and she keeps the schedule, so we all switched. Two of the other nurses were super mad at her, but she said she'd take their on-call for a couple days next time it came up, and they said okay."

So Patricia's alibi didn't actually cover her between eleven and eleven-thirty that night; in fact, she'd been later to work than she should have been, maybe twenty minutes, maybe the amount of time it took to clean herself up after a murder. But her time log said she'd clocked in at eleven twenty-five. A time log she controlled, for a night she'd assigned herself, knowing full well she'd likely be called in.

The angry wife's alibi going up in smoke, like a match to a bonfire.

"Would you be willing to testify to this in court if it helps to catch Jeffries's killer?" I asked.

Now her attention came back to me fully, with suspicion. "Why, are you suspecting Patricia?"

"No, nothing like that," I lied, and then smiled. "Just being very thorough at this point." I couldn't have her talking to the wife until the uniforms had a chance to bring her in.

She sighed, looked back at the clock. "Yeah, sure, I guess."

"Thanks," I said. "That's all I had. You can go check on your patient now."

She was down the hall before I even finished my sentence.

I found the ME in the basement of the city's tax building, where the morgue had been moved after flooding once too often in its previous location. The building made me think of Cherabino, with some pain. She'd been the first one to bring me here. She'd been the one to get me hooked on solving murders. And now she was serving papers for the PI agency I wasn't even at this week.

I pushed it aside in time to say hello to the medical

examiner, a lovely woman with a Jamaican lilt who'd always been kind to me, despite the rumors of the horrors of telepaths. As a medical examiner, she was thorough and well-trained, and according to Cherabino, her testimony always played well with a jury.

I felt a little awkward; normally I brought some kind of cookies or something to meetings like this, but this time I'd forgotten. This was also the first time I'd been down here by myself, and it bothered me. The long rows of metal storage for corpses gave off a low-level shriek in Mindspace, their quantum stasis fields playing badly with Mindspace waves, but what bothered me more was the two bodies, a man and a woman, lying completely naked on the metal tables at the center of the room. Each had significant damage, damage that had killed them, and looking at them out in the open like this, without any dignity at all, bothered me a lot.

"What can I help you with?" the ME asked me, amused at something. Probably me.

"Um, I'm here about the Isaiah Jeffries case."

She frowned for a minute, thinking, then said, "I'm sorry, Adam, but the body has already been released to the funeral home."

"I figured it would be. Um, I just had a couple of questions. I assume you'll need to look at notes?"

She stood up from her small stool and walked over to a tall metal filing cabinet, pulling out the second drawer and paging through until she found the right file. She closed it and came back over to the small desk near me, gesturing for me to take a seat in the extra chair.

I said, "Jeffries was drowned? Intentionally?"

She glanced over the notes she made. "There wasn't enough water in the lungs to indicate drowning. I included the details in the report. Cause of death was arrhythmia. Possibly related to electrical influence. The bruises aren't indicative of either intentional or unintentional action. He was submerged at the time, but I don't think drowning is indicated."

Oh, that's right. "You're ruling it an accident, with the electrocution. Like Branen wants you to."

"My findings are based on the evidence, not on whatever a lieutenant wants, I assure you. The victim had a high blood alcohol level. These things happen." She sat and thought; I could see the thoughts darting around her head like fish in a pond. "If it was a straightforward accident, he would have knocked the cooler device into the water with a hand or an arm. I'd expect to see burn marks from where the electricity entered the body. His skin would be wet. You'd see that closed loop first." She looked at me. "At least that's the typical presentation. We don't see that here, and you could argue that the device fell into the water some other way. Accident is still the best read of the evidence, either way."

I took a breath. Two. I'd been working this, I realized, completely on the feelings I'd gotten from the Mindspace crime scene. I had to connect the last few dots or my certainty wouldn't mean anything and maybe Branen would want to consider the whole thing an accident.

"There were bruise marks on the neck," I said.

"That's right."

"Like someone had tried to strangle him."

"But the hyoid bone wasn't broken, the windpipe was whole if shut. It wasn't a successful manual strangulation, and with the influence of the heated water, there's no guarantee the wounds were perimortem."

I paused for a moment. "How big were the hands that strangled him? The hand, if there was just one? Can you tell from the bruise marks? Would it have been the right size for a smallish woman? She's a nurse, so she's not weak, but she's not big either."

"I take it you have a suspect?"

I nodded.

She pulled out a piece of paper, what looked like tracing paper with pencil marks on it. "These are the bruises," she said. "Eight inches on a side at most, even given the curve." She folded the paper carefully, to the curve of a throat, place her own very small hand above it. The marks were too far apart to be made by her fingers.

She offered me the paper and I did the same. My hands, rough in places still from my time on the streets, were broad, with long fingers. Even along the curve, I couldn't make them comfortably fit into the marks either. If my thumb lined up, my pointer or index finger was out of alignment. Whoever had done this had mid-sized hands, with shorter fingers closer together. I tried to remember what kind of hands Ms. Arnold had and drew a complete blank.

"Were the bruises deep?" I asked, for something to ask. I handed the paper back, and she put it back in the folder.

"No, and they're more diffuse than you might expect. Like whoever held his throat couldn't keep a grip or push very hard."

That would line up with my vision but didn't prove anything. "What about angle?" I asked. "Was the person short? Can you tell exactly when the bruising happened?"

"No way of telling. He or she was standing next to the victim, above him, as near as I can tell, reaching down. As I said, it could easily have been earlier in the day, though."

"There we go," I said. Washington was out, then; he would have been about Jeffries's height, and I couldn't see the reporter letting a hostile cop stand above him and to the side. It occurred to me to ask, "How realistic do you think it is to classify this one as a murder?"

The ME shrugged. "I ruled it an accident for a reason. If you're determined, I can see the case for intentional death. Honestly, I collect the facts, other people argue them. If I was a betting woman though . . ."

"Yes?"

"I'd try to account for that bruising. Without a good explanation for it—and given its nonlethality—you don't have a case."

"Would a smallish woman be able to cause the bruising you saw?"

"I couldn't rule her out."

"Okay, then," I said. I stood up and thanked her. "I have a lot to think about."

The ME smiled. "Glad I could be helpful." Then she turned back to her work, and I, back to mine.

It felt odd to be doing this part alone. Very, very odd indeed.

But I also had to finish this. I had to.

It could be the wife's hands, right? It could. I told myself that I believed Washington when he'd said he hadn't laid hands on the man. I did. Mostly.

When I arrived back at the station, it was an hour before quitting time, but I went over to the dispatch desk to see what it would take to get the wife brought back in for questioning tomorrow. I had an hour, maybe two at most, before I'd definitely be done with my part-time hours for the week. Maybe I could get away with working overtime.

When I asked the dispatch officer about procedure, though, she laughed and said Patricia Arnold was already in the interview rooms, as it happened. She'd walked in a few hours ago at the door closest to Dispatch and asked the officer to speak with whoever was handling her case.

"Really?" I asked, unbelievingly.

"Really," the officer said, and laughed as she took the next call on her headset.

I shook my head and got on the ancient elevator again, its buttons so worn from years of use you couldn't read the numbers anymore, and waited for it to make its way down to the second basement.

The doors finally opened with a *ding*, and sure enough, Interview Room 3 had its light on, clearly full. The trouble was, I knew better than to interrupt an interview mid-session, even if I was kinda pissed that nobody had invited me to it. I knocked on the door to the recording room next door, feeling two minds behind it, one of them Freeman's.

The recording room's door opened, and Freeman said. "Come in, but stay quiet," he said. His mind added that he'd like to know where I'd been once this was all over.

I moved into the recording booth and looked through the one-way glass that appeared as a mirror in the interview room. It was only two feet wide, but that was enough to see Patricia Arnold, and the sound system clearly projected both her words and Branen's, the back of whose head I could see through the glass.

Wait, Freeman was here with me in the booth. Why was Branen in there and not Freeman? This had to be big.

I started paying attention.

". . . my husband's notes are very thorough," Patricia Arnold said with the even tone of someone who'd said this all at least twice before. "They point to several officers caught in wrongdoing that was known and approved by the higher-ups in your department. None of this is published yet, and the *Journal* editor isn't expecting it. I know because I've been working with him since the beginning, and believe me, his sources are significant and go far beyond what I've learned through your department."

Branen's body language didn't change. "We have reasonable suspicion of a major crime, and we've searched your apartment once already. Do you really expect me to believe we haven't found all of it by now?"

Patricia didn't flinch. "My husband was a paranoid alcoholic studying corruption in the police force. Do you really think he didn't have backup copies away from the apartment?" She put her hands flat on the table. "I'm not here to threaten you or cause trouble. In fact, I'm here for exactly the opposite reason."

That made me curious—and I reached out past Branen to try to connect with her mind. Telepathy got a lot less strong the farther you were away from someone, but she was still in my range, even if weaker as a result. I heard her words now slightly before she said them.

"I'm here to help you guys. There's some damaging stuff here, and we all know Isaiah had a tendency to dig up things nobody else could find."

"We know about your relationship with Kalb," Branen said, flatly. "You were involved in everything he knew. We will trace it back and find all of the details you're privy to."

She laughed, and it wasn't a pleasant sound. "Trust me, you don't have it all. Kalb likes to talk, but it's rumors. Isaiah was a slippery bastard, but he was a damn good reporter. He'd take a rumor and track it down to hard evidence. He'd find things nobody else could find, and he had sources you couldn't imagine." She took a breath. "None of that matters right now. What matters is I'll protect you guys and keep all of the information quiet. If you'll work with me." She'd used Kalb, like she'd use her husband's research here, she was thinking. She'd do whatever it took.

"You want us to… work with you?" Branen asked, skepticism in his voice.

"Yes," she nodded. "I'll protect you, and you'll protect me." She'd killed her husband, her mind supplied, but she had the leverage. "I'm going to be on the straight and narrow from now on, and I'm sure this department will do the same.

There's no point in dragging the past into this. It would be bad for everyone." Then she waited, and I could feel her nervousness. She had leverage, but not a huge amount, and even she didn't know where all of Isaiah's notes were. She was counting on the department to want the difficulty over with more than they wanted to drag her through a trial. Hopefully.

Branen paused for a long time—at least forty-five seconds. Maybe over a minute. Finally, he said, "That's what I thought you were going to say. I don't see any reason to pursue this any further. As far as I'm concerned, your husband drowned from alcohol-related causes. That being said, I can re-open this investigation at any time if I see reason to."

"I understand," Patricia said, and I could *feel* her relief, her joy at having talked her way out of trouble. Her satisfaction that she'd gotten what she wanted, dead husband and Kalb and escaping prosecution. She'd gotten it.

I pulled away, disgusted.

"We take care of our department," Branen said evenly. "See that you keep that in mind."

"Absolutely. I wouldn't expect any less," Patricia the murderer said, and got up to shake Branen's hand across the table.

He let her go, escorting her out with courtesy, his body language even and settled.

Fury rose up in me like a flood.

"That's not fair!" I cried out, unable to help myself. The words echoed in the small space of the recording room, echoed with an ugly loudness.

Freeman turned and spoke to the recording technician. "Can you give us a minute?" The technician, who wanted a break anyway, left. Then Freeman said to me, specifically, "It's been decided. We're done."

"But it's not right," I said. "She did it. Any idiot could see that she did it." Or, at least any telepath could. "It was there in implication. Really. If we can just . . ." I trailed off. She hadn't said it, had she? She hadn't said anything out loud that we could use.

"Implication doesn't solve cases or get them prosecuted," Freeman said.

"There has to be more evidence," I said, a little desperately, fury still riding me. "Someone else we can talk to. It isn't right she's getting away with it just because she has his notes. We should be taking those damn things and doing investigations on them anyway!"

Freeman stood there and looked at me. "You done?"

"It's not right," I said, intensely frustrated. "It isn't."

Freeman shook his head, the scar compressing with the movement. "Look. I've got two gang shootings, a stranger murder, a serial rapist, three armed robberies with major injuries, a hostage situation during a bank robbery in which a man ended up dead, oh, and a political killing left on the steps of the courthouse. And that's just what's on my desk right now."

"It doesn't mean she should get away with it!"

"Let's say you're right. Let's say she did it. You read her right, you got the real story, you're totally right. That doesn't mean we can prove a bit of it. Any defense attorney in the world will argue accident with the evidence we've got, and she didn't confess. If anything, her husband's notes open a whole can of alternate suspects. It will never—never—make it through the court system with any positive outcome. And let's say that it could. With a hundred hours of investigation, with enough work and effort, we get her. So what? Recidivism rates on spousal murders are almost none, and that's a hundred hours we could have spent catching somebody who might actually do it again."

I shook my head, violently.

"Realistically she won't do it again. She has the notes, she has the bargain, but she also knows we're watching her. Branen's made the right call. We don't have the resources, and taking her off the street does nothing. We'd all be better off if I spend that time taking down that serial rapist or that political killer. At least those might make a difference." That was the most words I'd ever heard at once from Freeman, possibly the most I'd ever heard him say. His tone was flat and cynical, and very very certain.

"You're giving up," I said.

Freeman looked me straight in the eye then. "That's not what I said. The brass says we're done. So we're done. And. There's good reason to be done, and more cases to prosecute. Whining about the fairness of it all does nothing to help anybody, much less your victim. You want to work with this department, that's how it works."

"That's not right," I said, one more time. I was deeply, deeply frustrated. But there was nothing in the face of his absolute certainty. His body language, his mind, said take it or leave it.

"That's life. That's police work," he said, and walked out.

◆

Frustrated, I exited into the hall, passing the recording technician on his way back, now smelling of smoke. I wanted a cigarette. Bad.

Then I stopped cold, three feet from the elevator, right behind Branen.

The doors had opened, revealing Commander Draco with Lieutenant Paulsen's hand on his shoulder, pushing him forward.

"Commander Draco," Branen said then. "If you'll step into Interview Three, we have some questions for you about your involvement in the recent thefts from our evidence room." And a half a dozen other crimes and corruption charges, his mind supplied along with anger; for all his outward cool, Branen was not happy at this situation from Draco. At least that much was justice, I told myself. At least that.

Draco set his jaw, and I felt a wave of rage from him—not rage at a false accusation, but rage at getting caught. "I outrank you," he said, pulling away from Paulsen into the open hallway.

"You absolutely do, sir," Branen said evenly. "Which is why Lieutenant Paulsen and I will both be there while we wait for the county Internal Affairs investigator. The captain will also make an appearance later." He was thinking it was too early, that he'd rather have waited for clearer evidence against Draco before moving, but Kalb had forced his hand.

Draco noticed me then. "Who are you?" he barked at me.

"Nobody, sir," I said, and ducked into the now-empty elevator and pushed the button.

The doors closed, and I breathed, furious. I was deeply, deeply frustrated with Patricia getting away with the murder of Jeffries. He hadn't been a nice guy, but he'd done good thing and his murder was just... he would never get justice, would he?

But the accusations against Draco, rumors though they were, had a full investigation in the works. Maybe that was enough. Maybe it'd have to be. Maybe Jeffries's work to expose the corruption had done that much.

It still didn't feel fair, damn it. It still didn't feel fair.

I showed up at the PI office late, well after dinner, still upset but with check in hand for the week. We had bills to pay, and Mindspace Investigations wouldn't stay open at this rate, even with me putting the paycheck into the bills. Maybe the office space had been a mistake. Maybe it had been a huge, shitty mistake. Maybe this all was.

When I opened the front door, a light was on towards the back. A second's attention identified Cherabino's mind in the space in front of me. "Hi," I said, just loud enough that I thought she could hear me. She was probably still pissed, but whatever. Today so was I.

I shrugged off my coat, put it on the hook in the reception

area, and heard a faint greeting back. I pulled my check out of the coat pocket then and moved to the back, where Cherabino was, in front of the desk that was hers, across from the neater one that was mine.

She looked tired and felt worse, like she hadn't slept in days.

"What?" I yelled at her, out of patience. "What aren't you telling me?"

That made her stand up and face me, setting her jaw. "I do *not* appreciate you yelling at me."

"I don't effing care!"

"Well, hooray for you. I just got a thousand ROCs for the agency! You get to care now!"

"Oh," I said, and took a breath. "How'd you get a thousand?"

"A client hired me to do some research for him," she said, and her mind was both proud and a little resentful. "You get paid?"

"Yeah," I said. "Yeah, I got paid for a shitty case and an even shittier ending. They're dropping the case, Cherabino. The wife's holding shit over their heads, and they're dropping the case. Just because he was an addict, and not a nice guy. It's not fair."

"Oh," she said, and leaned against the edge of her desk. "That does sound pretty crappy."

"They say I'm done. Done. And Freeman's backing them up. What about justice? What about doing the right thing, for crying out loud?"

"Yeah, well, they aren't all that interested in doing the right thing anymore, now are they?" she asked, and I knew her bitter tone was all about the police brutality charge—the trumped-up charge—that had ended her career. "At least you still get to work there."

"Trust me, you didn't miss anything. It's going to be a shit show tonight anyway." I sighed and took my own seat on the edge of my own desk, maybe three feet away from her. And then I told her about the Draco thing.

She whistled when I was done. "Holy crap. If IA is going after somebody so high up, they're serious about this corruption thing." She wondered, briefly, if she'd seen anything suspicious she should have reported.

"Yeah," I said. I was still frustrated, but now, mostly, mostly tired. "I wanted to solve it, Cherabino."

"I know." She got up and came over, putting her hand on my shoulder. She moved slowly enough I anticipated and shielded, just enjoying the feel of her hand. "It's the worst, when you can't finish it."

"It really is," I said, meeting her eyes. I felt that tension again, the memory of all the kissing we'd been doing as recently as a month ago. The memory of how she felt under my hands.

She felt it too, and pulled away. She picked up her jacket from the back of the desk chair, and said, carefully, "You hungry? You can tell me all about the case over dinner. Maybe I'll tell you about mine too."

I took her peace offering, reluctantly. "Yeah. Food is good, and we can actually afford something with both of us bringing stuff in. Maybe."

"We'll be okay, Adam. We really will. The clients will come."

I took a breath. "I hope so," I said. "I really, really hope so."

Thank you for reading. Readers like you make everything possible.

Find out more about Alex Hughes and her work and read excerpts, short stories, deleted scenes and more at http://www.ahugheswriter.com.

While you're there, sign up for the newsletter: http://www.ahugheswriter.com/email-signup. Newsletter members get all the information on new releases first, plus (approximately as often as I feel like it) they get free short stories and other goodies just for being part of the list.

Check out the rest of the Mindspace Investigations series:
Rabbit Trick (short story)
Clean
Payoff (novella)
Sharp
Marked
Vacant

Still can't get enough? Consider leaving a review. Reviews help other readers find stories they love and help the series grow.

Thank you again for reading!

About the Author

Alex Hughes, the author of the award-winning Mindspace Investigations series from Roc, has lived in the Atlanta area since the age of eight. She is a graduate of the prestigious Odyssey Writing Workshop, and her short fiction has been published in several markets including *EveryDay Fiction*, *Thunder on the Battlefield* and *White Cat Magazine*. She is an avid cook and foodie, a trivia buff, and a science geek, and loves to talk about neuroscience, the Food Network, and writing craft—but not necessarily all at the same time. You can visit her at Twitter at @ahugheswriter or on the web at www.ahugheswriter.com.

49692347R00062

Made in the USA
Lexington, KY
16 February 2016